RETIRED... AND I'M STILL TIRED

MUSINGS OF A GRUMPY OLD COOT

Acknowledgments

I wish to thank all those in my personal life who made this book possible.

Mr. Nick Productions, LLC
©2022 by Mr. Nick Productions, LLC

Copy Editor – R. Graham

Front cover art – Dr. Mayputz and Kristy Klein
Back cover and spine – Dr. Mayputz and Kristy Klein
Book layout – Kristy Klein / FifteenBlue.com

Photo of fisherman – Anonymous
Published by Mr. Nick Productions, LLC ©2022

This book was NOT written by a ghostwriter

ISBN: 979-8-218-00183-4

Dedication

To my beloved, late father. He intelligently questioned anything and everything about life and death. This book would have made him laugh. Unfortunately, he would have had additional queries after reading it. Sorry, Dad, I still don't have all the answers.

Preface

If only I had somehow attained financial security as a younger man - it would have been wonderful to retire earlier instead of nearer to sixty-five. I once had plenty of energy, education, and skills, but no time or money. Now I have the reverse. And, like me, many young men and women had *chutzpah*, sawed through life, and diligently saved sawbucks in hopes of someday retiring wealthy and healthy. But anticipated excitement for the big "pay-off" near the end of life may be delusional positivity because elderly retirement frequently becomes a comic tragedy and not "Yay! Now I can really start living."

I simply cannot do the same things I used to, nor with the same vigor. My wife of over four decades fondly winds me up by saying that it's "normal" aging. Fuck that! And fuck her, too.

Or maybe not. That's yet another department that seems to have suffered a shortfall, with its head member slowly petering out. Fuck me! I used to have 90-100% days; now I'm lucky to skate by on 50% while not exactly feeling or behaving like TV's former wonder dog, Rin Tin Tin. Previously I could perform *Life* at a high level with little sleep, little food, and little effort. Now it's a chore just to get up at night to pee. Holy Hell, I'm old and tired!

This is not my first bout in the squared circle of the writing realm. Some readers may have already indulged in my previous literary offerings and hopefully found them enjoyable. Although loosely based on lifelong recollections and observations, this *ageist* book is "technically" fictional. It is a book of humorous musings and should be taken as such. There is no malicious intent; the only intent is to entertain!

Dr. I. Mayputz
My preferred pronouns are: he/she/it/cuzz/bro/dude

Table of Contents

Introduction

I am not a medical doctor, a psychologist, or even a sociologist but an insignificant former pharmacist and newly retired dentist. After a lifelong struggle with a chronic illness and job-related stress, I thought a comedic book on the various aspects of aging might be in order. Though not strictly a memoir, my intentions were to slightly relive my life while poking a little fun at the absurd promises made to senior citizens about the "good" times ahead. At the same time, I want to give hope and encouragement to the many "wounded pensioners" out there who have almost given up on a "normal" existence. However, even in retirement, the battles continue. It seems as if the processes of aging and slowing down are not a panacea or as therapeutically rewarding as originally hoped for. What the hell? I was tired while working and I'm still tired, dammit! Retirement was supposed to be a

"lifetime achievement award," a decadent dessert or a "gravy train" after a life of hard work. But, instead, it congealed into lumpy gravy, at best. The golden years somehow turned into rusty ones. Let's explore what happens after you lock up for the last time. Hopefully you will find the stories within the following pages to be humorous and not overly tiring, and you will laugh along with me. Maybe at me, as well!

Enjoy.

Dr. I. Mayputz

1

Be Careful What You Wish For!

Ah, the dreams of mice and men - I mean rats. The dirty rats keep on living while the meek and mild mice succumb. Is that really true? And which rodent do I resemble in retirement? Rats, I refuse to answer that question! As an impressionable teenager I remember raptly listening to my old man at the dinner table, especially when he was rattling on about a dearly departed fellow professor from his civil engineering department. "He was just sixty-five years old and kicked the bucket," Pop lamented as yet another one of his close, elderly co-workers died an "early" death. "He retired last week and told everyone! And he didn't even collect any Social Security. And he and his wife had so many plans, too," said Dad rather glumly as he shook his head in disgust. Life just wasn't fair. It was almost as if Murphy's Law was at play: the more you looked forward to something, the less likelihood you had of attaining it. And conversely, did the rascally, rapscallion types of professors "get away" with being louts and lousy lecturers but kept right on ticking way past their supposed expiration dates? You know it! However, was it all genuine comedic karma or did it just seem that way? "He wanted to go to nude beaches, sleep in late and drink Cruzan Rum all day," sputtered Pop after yet another recent collegiate retiree bit the dust. But I will tell you that after a few of those unfortunate workplace-related incidents, Dad only reluctantly and sporadically spoke about any grandiose plans he may have had for his future after retiring. He wasn't about to foolishly jinx his life that way. He was determined not to tempt the Fates; no way! Instead, he very quietly ended his thirty-plus year tenure at the college in our hometown without hubris or fanfare. He was sixty-five on the button and ready to vacate. He previously had his pension, health insurances, Social Security payouts and Medicare all meticulously figured out. Then he shook hands with his officemate, took one last look around his immaculate cubicle, strode through his office door for the last time, and walked down one hill and up another to our house. It's as if it was a normal Friday evening and nothing unusual had transpired. The last three decades of his storied teaching career were now an afterthought. And he wanted it that way; he was cautious and superstitious as hell! Wouldn't you be, too? After officially retiring, he designed and built my sister's and my house, played plenty of competitive tennis, and journeyed to many countries abroad, even to his beloved Estonia from whence he had emigrated as a youngster. He also got to vacation multiple times in St. Croix, Mexico, and the Bahamas, as well as cruise the Caribbean. Although always playing

it close to the vest, he had a long and grand
retirement, at least as seen through the eyes of
his favorite, only son. However, I never had
the chance to really question him on his senior
wishes and desires. I had heard persistent and
whispered family rumors that he wanted to
relocate to southeastern Florida and fish in
perpetuity, but that pipe dream never
materialized. I guess he had never hooked
Mom with that kind of reasoning. Perhaps he
died at ninety-one still dreaming of something
else which he would never divulge out loud
for fear of it backfiring. Maybe my mom
knows, but she's not talking either; she just
misses him dearly. Was Dad a mouse or a rat?
I don't know, but he seemed to have navigated
admirably through life without stirring up
wonton bad luck like the arrogant and foolish
Fool in the Tarot deck of cards. However, Pop
may have benefitted from strong genetics, too.
His father had passed away at age ninety-nine.
Perhaps some snippets of that DNA are in me

as well. Let's think positively, but not rock the boat - and not plan too far ahead, either!

2

Spirituality, Piety, or Hedonism?

Simply put, spirituality acknowledges suffering, piety embraces it, and hedonism seeks to avoid it at all costs! And the age-old conundrum on how to live one's life is influenced by family, friends, environment and heredity. But now that retirement is here, can retirees effectively reverse the previously dominant paradigms, shed established dogmas and finally feel free to fuck around, or to join a latter-day cult? Or, to embrace age-old, as well as New Age, adulterated, Buddhist spiritual teachings? Maybe. Most working stiffs didn't have the luxury of time to adequately examine their lives in depth while mired in debt, marital woes, child-rearing, etc. LIFE can effectively thwart any meaningful evaluation of LIFE. However, retirees seem to have more seconds on the clock and perhaps they can reflect on, and possibly extricate themselves from, some of the stagnant ruts they fell into all those younger years ago. But is it always a rewarding and joyous quest to suddenly discover that you had messed up your so-called entire existence, at least as compared to your idyllic Facebook and Instagram fiends (that word is spelled correctly)? Ha! An existential crisis can hit anyone, anytime, regardless of age. However, contemplating morbidities and mortality become pressing and depressing endeavors as the geriatric set desperately realizes that there are upcoming and inevitable expiration dates! But can seniors really change things around for the better in a Goddamn hurry? My wife and I have hundreds of self-help volumes embarrassingly lining our family room's built-in bookshelves. There are the requisite Dyer, Tolle, Ruiz, Lao Tzu, Confucius, and others, all having been read at least once, but now gathering dust. They are all there, however. We even have books on the personality enneagram, mystical shamanism, Prada, universal energy, brain health, and Reiki. Hottie Blondie (my wife's nickname since our mutual pharmacy college days) and I are also certified, advanced level, Reiki practitioners. Perhaps we are both just certifiable? Anyway, no matter whose literature you read and digest, they all seem to imply similar and universal axioms. And they are: Mindfulness, acceptance, patience, empathy, community, and exercise. I may have left out a few saliant tenets, but you get my point. Now, I don't mean to demean these ancient, as well as copy-cat, manuscripts of wisdom. But should we now wholeheartedly reach out and find solace and guidance by adulating Tony Robbins and his mesmerizing oratories and writings? Are we to be duped in our dotage while trying to grasp at spiritual salvation straws because our time is almost up? Perhaps, and maybe it is a natural progression of mind over matter. We now have the experience of horrible hindsight, and a cogent word here and there coming out of Covey or Carnegie could really help. How could it hurt, right? Well, maybe in the pocketbook or if you join a Dianetics science! Or at least until the next must-have book comes out when you will have to retool your thinking yet again. I can honestly tell you that mentally devouring these types of books for years has helped my wife and I to think outside the box. However, reality still creeps in; it is damn hard to practice what "they" preach! Becoming more religious, or at least to acknowledge a higher power, is another step that some retired folk step into. Most mainstream religions have been built on exactly the kinds of mindful teachings just talked about. Some retirees reach that kind of spiritual awakening, but with a god at the podium. Kind of like starting to go to church to hob-nob with like-minded souls and then comforted by looking forward to a pleasant, ghostly afterlife. But what if you hate people? What if humans have so destroyed your trust in them that they now only serve as a source of fetid aggravation? Nobody mentions THAT in religious texts, at least not explicitly. Starting to "believe" again is nice but that could possibly only extend your unpleasant suffering here and now before you embark on a potential heavenly sojourn. However, according to some non-flat-earth scientists, the world will physically end in billions of years after the sun runs out of hydrogen. Then it will become a red giant and engulf the first three planets in its way, including puny Earth. Will heaven also be erased in that cosmic calamity? I don't know, which leads us to the last salvation of seniority, salacious as it may sound: enough with the endless suffering; let's have more fun while we can, period! Perhaps finally enjoying the fruits of labors, tasting hitherto forbidden fruit and expounding on previously fruitless desires are the ways to go? Bygone passions, hobbies, sports, etc. can now be rekindled and ramped up if there is the physical and mental wherewithal to do so. So burned out minds and muscles are not what they once were. So, what. Burn or donate most of the accumulated "healing" books and start sweatin' to the oldies! Where is Richard Simmons when you need him most? I guess even he is too old and fat to gyrate any longer. Oh well. Anyhow, now is the time to seize the day and to stop whining about never being rewarded for seemingly endless hardworking and wholesome lives. My wife reminds me daily to stop complaining! Life is often unfair and there may not be a godly judge to praise the rank and file and to promise a Kingdom Come. Remember, there are no tangible awards for the *mensches* in the trenches. Most folks obediently went to work, raised ungrateful brats, and sent humongous taxes to a dysfunctional government, and then paid

the ultimate price by growing old in the tooth.
Good lord! And grief, regrets,
disillusionments, and disappointments
accrued too, and those debilitating feelings
cannot easily be erased by pensions or
Medicare. Nothing about becoming older is
easy - nothing. However, I believe it's time to
live a little, if possible. Rather than meekly
exploring hidden agendas, perhaps we should
finally act on them? And I don't mean blowing
up hurtful habits like addictive gambling and
drug abuse, but engaging in MORE exercise
and sexual hijinks. Maybe elderly couples can
start willful "camping" again? Why not? With
a little pharmaceutical help, men can once
again pitch tents and put poles in holes.... I
mean if geriatric Suzanne Somers can
supposedly have sex three times per day with
her dullard husband, why can't the rest of the
retired *schlubs* out there? Granted, they admit
to consuming and injecting a shitload of
chemicals, some illegal, to keep "things"

lubricated and pointed in the right direction. But, hey, at least they are trying! By contrast, what are most old men doing, just barely holding on while holding their own? And womenfolk? Do most senior ladies close-up shop, throw out razors, and mentally check out? Please, say it ain't so! Now is the time for more carnal cornucopia, I think. There are even anecdotal reports that nursing home couplings are on the upswing. I guess there is nothing else left to do in there but to free willy! But it's easy to be encouraging and gloss over the loss of libido, spouses, and lovers. Cell senescence, cancer, chronic illnesses, obesity, and psychological trauma can also put dampers on feisty frivolity. And if you can hardly get off the couch to feed yourself, or to urinate, getting frisky with a paramour may be more trouble than it's worth. Enough said. However, perhaps a wee bit of naughty hedonism coupled with an aware, mindful heart can go a long way to bolster oldsters against the obvious ravages of retirement. And I mean mindful, not mind full, which is yet another unpleasant reality of aging.

3

BMI and TMI

My longtime nephrologist and cardiologist continually say that I am overweight. They both independently state that I look good for my "retired age" and am now classified as obese instead of morbidly obese, according to their actuarial death tables. My mother-in-law, Sandi, heard me spouting off about my recent medical appointments while she was seated at the kitchen table during a recent holiday visit. She is a short, rather plump, non-trans woman. Not porky, just a bit portly. She had had a few too many vodka highballs, the norm for her, put down her glass, looked up at me and hollered, "You're fuckin' obese?" Then she lifted her shirt up above her bra and shouted, "This is fuckin' obese! Give me a fuckin' break. You look great. Your foreign doctors are fuckin' idiots!" I glanced at her grossly distended belly and just nodded in tacit agreement. I really didn't want to see that, but it was just too late. However, I thanked her for thinking that I was a hunky, masculine man. She nodded back. She always had a good eye when eyeballing handsome heterosexual males, and I appreciated that. That sentiment was not lost on my wife who suddenly kissed me, as if corroborating her mom's taste in *hot* men. Winning, or maybe not. My two doctors are ethnic Tunisian and Indian, respectively, and both are tall, gaunt, Vegan, bean poles. Neither of them smoke, drink, dance nor chew. Although they appreciate my physicality and elite athleticism, in their minds I am still over the limit and way too fat! In their respective "books" I need to lose fifty pounds, at least, if not more. But how? I am still off their medical charts, regardless of my ongoing dieting efforts and supposed sports prowess. It's Goddamn mentally fatiguing counting empty calories and reluctantly gazing in the mirror only to see an unfamiliar and flabby old fart. Hey, that's me, darn it! I used to be so young and dashing - well at least young. But Hottie Blondie thinks I still have potential; she has been willingly married to me for almost four decades. However, does that really count? When a longtime spouse compliments you for being her cat's meow, regardless of your portliness, is it just a formulaic and kind remark to keep the status quo? It's hard to tell. It could go either way. I know she means well and perhaps only wants to harden things up. It may be her cunning plan to keep stroking my fragile male ego, and other things, while stoking the sexual chemistry betwixt us. But now as a retiree, with more "free" time on my hands to finally get fit, that damn aging process is getting in the way of my renewed, but seemingly sophomoric, efforts. For me, daily strenuous workouts and dieting are tiring, not quite good enough, and not rejuvenating endeavors at all. But I'm not a triathlete, I'm a do-athlete, dammit! However, I still find myself flailing and failing at times. I've tried, even so far as becoming a certified, part-time, personal *fitness* trainer years ago. It didn't matter then and still doesn't. Maybe it's because I never abused illicit compounds, like the majority of "fit pikers" do in the sordid and fraud-filled fitness industry? Anyhow, as an AARP magazine recipient, I have the hours but no longer the body that can be effectively molded and sculpted back into shape. Like a *bad* piece of clay in a Claymation movie, it is lumpy, clumpy and uncooperative. Nevertheless, perhaps I should gracefully accept my imperfections, genetics and limitations, instead choosing to be present, grateful, and patient. I realize that I'm on a protracted *Highway to Hell* (my wife's and my actual AC/DC wedding song) but it's not over yet. Therefore, I should probably graciously accept my ongoing obesity while knowing am mere inches away from

so.

4

"I'll Do It, But My Heart Ain't in It!"

A familiar sentiment, I do believe. Most teenagers "picked" a college/job at seventeen or eighteen while being hornswoggled by an incompetent high school misguidance counselor (if he was so smart, why was he only a lowly guidance counselor?). It had been a hurried five-minute meeting during the fall of senior year and now the future was supposedly all planned out and happily set forever. What the fuck? How do I know? It happened to me and I'm sure it occurred to many others, as well. Now, I'm fairly certain that a few smart-ass kids had "life all figured out", but the vast majority of acne-faced, *scut-monkeys* just barely bumbled through reform school (high school) or BOCES and needed to be given some sort of directions for adulthood. And it was ALWAYS about making money down the road. Following your passion was not an option for most; God forbid! I mean, unless you could play the fiddle like virtuoso Itzhak Pearlman or swim like multiple Olympic gold medal winner Mark Spitz, then maybe most high school dorks did need some type of directed supervision. Otherwise, they all would have moved back in with parental units and done nothing, kind of like today's "geriatric-retired" and *woke* millennials. Anyway, most newly degreed doofuses in my dinky village grabbed their diplomas and went to community colleges, the farm, or to work at the local NAPA store/Cumby gas station. Remember, making the moola was of paramount importance. Neither mine or my friends' families were rich enough to subsidize and house a "starving artist" or unemployed lawyer. However, did any of us begrudgingly and unwittingly make the right choices as bewildered teenagers, kind of like Mikey in the Life Cereal commercial? Much to the

surprise of his brother and friend, he ate the cereal after initially being skeptical about it. "He likes it, hey Mikey" was the ad's positive punchline. Was my punchline a seemingly contented four-score prosthodontic imprisonment and am I now just a whining and wealthy dental "ex-con"? It's possible, even probable. Many greenhorn high school graduates tried college or working and then being happy with their chosen lots, but shouldn't it have been the other way around? Shouldn't happiness in the selection of a vocation come first? Back in *shul* many desperate hombres had desperately sought career and life guidance from television, family, and friends during the drug-addled '70s. Laugh-In, Hee Haw, and Walter Cronkite were some of the celebrity and cerebral instructors back then. In addition, my friends and I went so far as to try long hair, polyester bellbottoms and dimwitted Disco to help ease the pain of not knowing how to best mold our futures; including how to get a high paying job that was liked! It wasn't easy, though. Inadvertent mistakes were made. For instance, most guidance counselors weren't psychologists or even rocket scientists. Mine was a former agriculture teacher that could finish milking a Holstein cow one-handed in five minutes flat – his record was emblazoned on a plaque near the main office door on the first floor of my bovine-inspired, rural high school. THIS was the guy giving ME advice? Sheesh. However, perhaps I had been fortunate. Maybe I was well suited for my eventual profession all along and ended up less miserable than some of my boyhood pals. Nonetheless, many adults often slog thru life while ensconced in dead-end and frustratingly mindless, soul-sucking avocations while anxiously awaiting death or retirement, whichever comes first. But wait a minute. What about a retirement mulligan and a chance for a do-over, to get it right this time around? Oh, retirement, the chance to finally unwind, to take a Fresh Step and pursue a new and fulfilling job. Or to at least indulge full-time in a favorite pastime and then see if you can milk it for money? It all sounds so peachy keen and doable, but is it practical or logical? And is making a boatload of Benjamins still necessary? Boy, all these thoughts for a senile old coot like me to consider... maybe demented delusions CAN finally come true in old age? I personally know of numerous people who have ditched pent-up "unpleasantries" AFTER their working lives were ostensibly over. They shed wives, kids, cars, careers, etc. for the sake of life, liberty, and the pursuit of happiness with upgrades, such as acquiring new flames and revamped financial plans. Starting from scratch is nothing new and can be done, but there is frequent collateral carnage that can occur with that kind of egotistical chicanery. Conversely, many of my close male chums stuck it out with the same old bags, a steady stream of six-cylinder eggbeaters and the same old keys to the same old office doors. Maybe they are just happy with the same old routines? Or maybe life threw them a few curve balls that could not be hit, and they settled on a strike-out? Nobody had warned them that newfound mental and physical infirmities amid ongoing chronic illnesses would be a bitch to bear and hard to overcome. How can one start anew if there is no tiger in the tank anymore? Sure, there are some like my mom, who switched gears from being an unhappy doormat housewife to a tenured college professor in midlife. Then she happily retired and did not start anew in a totally different occupation. However, most people wait patiently to strike after an all-consuming day job is no longer needed. But do some wait too long? Can success and happy times, while rutting around in a brand-new workplace, finally rain down on elderly folks during retirement? Maybe so. I had originally tried pharmacy, hated it, and then settled on dentistry. I did alright and was good at the tooth game, or so some people inferred. Mine was a four-decade-long stint of daily dental horseshit, but I made a good coin and left the field marginally satisfied. I had the manual dexterity to wrangle wayward molars and canines, and even got handsomely rewarded for it. However, upon candid reflection, I realize that non-paying sports and writing are my real loves, besides my wife. Wow, isn't that a kick in the kimono? But there is no renumeration for those mentioned hobbies and habits unless you are the best of the best, and frankly, I am not. I also recall having been a somewhat talented musician (piano) and tennis player back in the day. Should I have pursued either as a livelihood or now rekindled them as satisfying wage earners in retirement? Or would I have ended up teaching forehands to retired little old ladies for minimum wage at some nondescript country club as a "pro" or given keyboard lessons as an underpaid music teacher at my alma mater? Or should I have pursued my youthful passion for nature and the creepy crawly animals within? I don't know. In retrospect, no one put a gun to my head to become a dentist, but maybe someone should have so I might have stopped! Anyway, I had swallowed any boyish aspirations, did the "right" thing as far as a career goes, and somehow "made it" to some semblance of retirement. But was much of my stressful professional life's resultant largesse and supposed success a result of plain dumb luck? Of course! And is starting over again in another field as a retired and tired old man the new plan? I don't think so. I don't care if my mom did it so effortlessly. However, come to think of it, how can teens really know what they are good at? And is it any different for old duffers? I look in the mirror and see a bona fide, craggy oldster leering back, one that tries to convince me that I still have it. But thank God I don't have to make bank by throwing the javelin, running paltry USATF age-group races, or winning inconsequential pickleball tournaments. I guess dentistry has been fruitful and kind to me after all. I managed to save a few doubloons and should probably shut the fuck up and stop wailing. Oh well; a toast to my fellow old fogies, some of whom are enjoying a fabulous, work-related second wind, and not just farting from eating too many vegetables. And a hearty handshake to those who miraculously got it right the first time and are still grunting away like pigs in shit, pushing pills, teaching school, or selling automobile parts and, smiling from hearing aid to hearing aid. And a shout out to people like me, who aspired for a few things, did a few others, and still got to home plate safely. However, I have no intention of starting a new vocation. Personally, I'm not too pooped to mount my wife, but just too tired to mount another furious charge and try some radical, modern job this late in life. Career-wise, and in my mind, I am 0 for 2. Nonetheless, things sort of worked out for me. I ended up practicing prosthodontics, but my heart wasn't always in it. To sum up, I think I'll stay functionally retired and not worry about a third go-round in yet another field. For emotionally and physically fatigued frumps like me, maybe reading the daily newspaper, thinking about exercise and sometimes lounging around in a bathrobe while scouring Facebook and Instagram is good enough. Hopefully Medicare, Social Security, and pension plans will not be eliminated any time soon, and I can finally decide how to truly be happy. And maybe, just maybe, Mr. T., my high school guidance counselor, wasn't such a homespun *nudnik* after all when he conscientiously got the education ball rolling and snookered me into initially attending

pharmacy college in early September 1977.
Perhaps he saw some kind of potential in me
after all, or plain got lucky.

5

Second Helping

No, I didn't maliciously rip off Lynyrd Skynyrd and its 1974, wildly popular, second studio effort. In fact, I have that exact vinyl album in my eclectic and extensive collection of Rock 'n Roll LPs! It sits next to my Boston and Badfinger records. I just thought that title might be apropos for this vignette, basically expounding on the previous one. Some people retire early, such as from the Military or the State, replace their worn shoe-tops, and then plunge headlong into a different, full-time career. Some leave and then return to the same desk, albeit part-time for another go round. Many take off and resurface as wobbly Price Chopper greeters, just for a few bucks and to get out of the house. And some take the two-count, quit their day jobs, move to the Bahamas, turn up the country music and wallow in the shallow sea in front of their beachfront home all day, every day (I personally know a retired couple like that, and both are long-retired ex-cops)! However, numerous folks take the three count and die, having never retired in the traditional sense at all. There are varying paths on the way to "retirement" and beyond. After reaching that "magical age," which is undoubtedly different for everyone, some people keep occupationally working, at least in a limited capacity. And some choose to stay home and play pickleball on their backyard courts, at least during the summers. Anyway, when I was just starting out as a young dental associate without a practice, I mutually hooked up with a locally popular and "super-successful" older dentist. He promised me the world and I had fanciful thoughts of taking over his large and lucrative practice in a time-honored and honorable transfer of power between two dental equals. Ha! It never happened. And no written contract had been signed, either. His constant lying and greed (he would have sold his own elderly mother for a buck) finally bubbled over after a year of dentate purgatory as I slowly realized that he would never relinquish his cash cow - ever! Later, as an accomplished and well-established prosthodontist with my own large and successful offices, I learned that he had passed away at age eighty-six, still drilling away five-days-per-week while continually promising the moon and the stars to naïve recent dental graduates. Reliable rumors circulated that he worked on a Monday and died that evening. But that's one way to NOT retire – just keep grinding away on that same grindstone until you can't grind anymore! Now, contrast that kind of work ethic and money-grubbing fortitude with my old man's. My professor father taught civil engineering at the college in my hometown. It had been a great gig for him: summers off, nights and weekends off, paid holidays, personal days off, no mandatory overtime, but meager wages as compared to private industry salaries. However, the retirement bennies were most excellent. Lifetime health insurance (besides Medicare), and two generous State pensions besides Social Security, all kicked in together at age sixty-five. Bonus! He put down his Slide Rule, chalk, and eraser, cleaned out his office, officially retired, and never looked back. He could easily have stayed, however, because no one forced him out. He had been a long-tenured and beloved full professor, but quit as soon as the clock struck sixty-five. There were some forays made by the university to have him return on a part-time, per diem basis, but he didn't want or need a second stint. He was certainly fit enough mentally and physically, though. However, he mentioned over and over that he had had enough of all the manufactured collegiate intrigues and bullshit and did not need the "blood money." And he never went back, not

even to visit, although the college was a mere
five minutes from our house. Who knew that
teaching college students for just over three
decades had been so exhausting for him?
Anyhow, my mom was also a college professor
at the same fine institution. She had been a
very popular French and Spanish instructor
and retired shortly after Pop did. But she got
bored and was instantly rehired, on a part-
time basis, and lasted another ten years with
the university being grateful for her lecturing
services. The college brass hated to finally see
her leave as she reluctantly vacated at long last.
However, she had willingly come back for a
second helping and loved it. By middle-age,
my pharmacist wife left the harried chain gang
at CVS and never looked back. That was quite
enough, and she gracefully bowed out. But it
was the right decision for her. And me? After
selling my last dental practice in 2011, I
became a part-time, hired gun, employee
prosthodontist (restorative dental specialist)

for large, area dental offices. Then my drilling days dwindled down to one-per-week and even that was unnecessarily stressful at times. Encroaching infirmity, a slow diminution of my senses, and a lifetime of putting up with dysfunctional staff members and unappreciative patients also contributed to my surliness and impatience. I was a well-seasoned dental specialist although the fickle and ambivalent, yet demanding, public gave me no quarter. But that's life in the toothy fast lane and even as a semi-retired dental *schmuck* I didn't fit in anymore. I already had my day in the dental sun, made some good *gelt* and it was high time I walked off the field. Now I am ostensibly disengaged from that dental drill, for better or worse. Do I miss dentistry? Perhaps a bit, but only a little. Sure, I fill in occasionally for the young and handsome dentist whom I worked for, so I guess I still have my gloved hands in it, so to speak. However, has my work-life ending been right for me? I don't know because I have been retiring slowly for quite some time. Nevertheless, I cannot see myself in a forty-hour-per-week position ever again. It's a strange phenomenon but I just can't do it full time anymore. However, unlike my dad, I will most likely keep going back for seconds, thirds, etc., especially if the bites are small and spaced out between feedings. But for now, there is more time for alleged comedic writing, fitness, real estate management, and sports. Spending more time cavorting with my wife in the Bahamas and Baja is also a possibility. Things could be worse.

6

Naptime

Whether a result of poor sleeping habits or being ragged-out from old age, scheduled napping seems to be a normal part of the day for many retirees. But is this behavior normal or even desirable? Are senior citizens genuinely tired, bored, or do they desperately need to catch a few winks before resuming their action-packed Facebook scrolls? Intuitive rest, like our pre-Industrial Revolution relatives practiced, is no longer in vogue or desirable in the modern world. Not even as a mid-day siesta as per former Mexican culture, I'm afraid. So, what are senior A-listers to do? Take a powder, take a break, and take a nap, that's what! The list of world-renowned luminaries who have intentionally taken somnolent interludes and bragged about them is long and legendary. However, some medical soporific specialists insist that cleaning up sleep-hygiene patterns and having relaxing bedtime rituals are preferable to nodding off on the couch in broad daylight, even while watching titillating shows on the boob tube. Some even say that daytime narcoleptic napping is a pathology and urgently needs to be medicinally addressed. Maybe so. In truth, there are many serious conditions, including sleep apnea, chronic illnesses, obesity, and persistent pain, that are major contributors to poor nightly somnolence and should be medically monitored. But what about pre-planned dozing, as previously mentioned? Margaret Thatcher, the Iron Lady of England, reportedly slept no more than four-hours-per-night, but took a "refreshing" daily snooze in the afternoon. Eleanor Roosevelt was rumored to have "checked-out" and napped before major speeches. Albert Einstein supposedly slept for ten hours and then "sawed wood" some more during his thought-provoking days. He would drift off in the afternoons in his favorite chair, but not as imagined. It was reported that he held an object in his hand that would fall as he started snoring. The noise would wake him before he reached the second stage of sleep. The first stage was all that he wanted: full of vivid imagery, creativity, and deep insights. Salvador Dali basically did the same thing throughout his eccentric, painter's life. Thomas Edison had a different approach. He was fond of boasting that he only needed four hours of shut-eye per night and then craftily crept away during the day as needed to sneakily slumber on fold-out bunks that he had strategically positioned in his home and laboratories. My own widowed, paternal grandfather, who lived with my family after he sold his house and retired, made a big deal about announcing his sacrosanct and daily lie-downs after lunch. My old man would also come home from professorial lecturing at midday and take a power nap on the living room sofa. Mom matter-of-factly stated that he would awaken refreshed and was more than ready to "teach" the progressive, liberal-minded, long-haired, anti-war, hippie freaks in his classes all afternoon. It was the late sixties, you know. Anyway, for years Dad had "religiously" listened to combative and conservative radio news host Bob Grant out of his earpiece every weekday at midnight and that most likely contributed to his daytime sleepiness! Anyhow, during my last years of working full-time, I also found it "necessary" to indulge in a ritualistic naptime on most days. Fortunately, I was practicing close to home and could scoot to my house during lunchtime for a quick bite and bedding. So, what is the takeaway from this longwinded tirade? Are we oldsters destined to relive kindergarten once more, when we were forced to lie down for a half hour on fold-out, blue cots after lunch? Or maybe our encroaching *lifestyles* and ongoing diseases have begun to dictate our lives, and we HAVE to take rests whenever possible? Regardless, I believe there is no right or wrong and perhaps simply having more free time to nod off, regardless of infirmity, is one of the luxuries of retirement. Damn the sickness, lack of energy, and retired tiredness; sometimes it just feels so good to hit the pillow anytime, anyplace! "If it feels good, do it!" started out as a naïve, leftover, progressive battle cry from Woodstock that morphed into a sardonic, hedonistic rejoinder and a nihilistic referendum on life. In essence: I'm going to die anyway so I might as well live it up now. But let's not delve too deeply into psychological dictums - if a nap feels good, do it!

7

Dieting or Dying?

I have tried most "diets," yet remain a fat boy. And true to form, my wiseacre adult son affectionately and appropriately calls me *Phatboy*. I retort by teasingly calling him an ectothermic animal: one that eats very little, expends little energy, and regulates its body temperature based on the surroundings. Lowly fish and amphibians are good examples. Actually, he is in great shape, works out regularly and eats intuitively, whereas I live to eat and not the other way around. However, in my shriveled and elderly mind I am still an enthusiastic and energetic sportsman. In fact, I was a FORMER, many-times over, local tennis champ and the past winner of four international snowshoe sprint events. However, now I feel like a slowed-down, hard-shelled, old box turtle. I have just enough fast twitch muscle fibers remaining in my arms and legs to effectively compete in watered-down sports or to do the "turtle" should I land on my back. Nevertheless, despite my slowly expanding handicap of bodily heft, I can still raise a paddle or two and squash unwitting ping pong balls and pickleballs coming in my general direction. But perhaps I am exaggerating a bit about my portly countenance and codgerly nature to make a point: most people do not age gracefully, and that unsightly stomach bulge is not the exception, but the rule! A silent majority of senior citizens gradually put on poundage, albeit some more than others. Most were serious working stiffs in their heydays and seriously went to work, worked seriously, and paid little heed to the cellulite creeping up their thighs and caboose. Plus, there was never enough time or willingness to exercise or eat right. And the rampant fast-food industry "conspired" to not only supersize people but

to keep everyone coming back for "free"
fill-ups. The food pyramid was all wrong, too.
Wonder Bread should have been placed at the
top (to be eaten sparingly) and Spam at the
bottom. Who knew? And I won't get into all
the Tang, cyclamates, and sodium nitrites that
were also consumed with relish. But let's stick
to fat - at least human fat. Retirement should
give people pause – not diapause which is a
form of stuporous invertebrate hibernation
– and the opportunity to reflect upon the
great harms that have been perpetrated on
older bodies and minds, and to change course.
Because if not now, when? Now is the time to
correct the errant ways and sail off into the
sunset in good shape and in wonderful health
– just like that elderly couple does while on
their sailboat, featured in old Centrum Silver
commercials. Yeah right! Anyway, even
"informed" citizens accumulated excess
tonnage from pounding savory and greasy
burgers, and don't forget the salty fries.

Nevertheless, all is not lost. No, there are a ton of diets to choose from to help the helpless shed unwanted physical baggage. And besides slimming outward silhouettes, it appears that losing weight also greatly lessens bodily inflammation. Less circulating cytochines, cortisol, bradykinins, metalloproteases, histamines, prostaglandins, insulin, etc., seem to decrease various acute and chronic disease states. Wow. I gotta put down that bucket of fried chicken and grab a cobb salad instead. Or eat the cob and not the corn kernels. Or at least fill up on homemade corn pone and not store-bought corn chips! Alas, we now know how we got here, but can we really transform ourselves into all those slender, full-of-life, white-haired "TV commercial people?" Are they for real? Give me a fuckin' break; ain't acting grand?! Anyway, as opposed to mainstream Hollywood hooey, my journey toward "wellness" as a retiree has been filled with many twists and sorry turns. Although I had managed to squeeze in tennis at an elite level while performing an exhausting and numbing (pun intended) day job (dentistry - basically performance art with a smattering of biological science thrown in), my weight slowly crept up regardless of the time spent on the court. And although I was rather muscular and participating in rigorous and competitive sporting events as a newly minted retiree, my blood pressure kept rising, and I felt ever more ungainly when moving through space. Plus I was still eating everything in sight. Was that the real problem? Possibly. However, my increased heaviness was not sudden; the protruding beer belly took decades to ferment and come to fruition. Hey, maybe it was all genetics? My parents were rather stocky humans, as well as their immediate Estonian ancestors. Perhaps I was screwed from the get-go. Was it my wife's fault? Was it her cunning culinary cuisine that had unfortunately blown me up? Notwithstanding,

SHE looks and feels great, at least whenever I feel her up. So, what was my problem? Was it the ageist trope that normally savvy seniors dread to hear – "normal fatty aging from eating and drinking too much?" Fuck that! Well, not one to sit on my duff, except when writing, paying bills, or defecating, I decided to take a different approach to wellness. Athletics and exercise were fine and dandy, however, it was the nutrition traversing my cake hole that needed fine tuning! So, I made up my mind NOT to get rid of the alcoholic "suds," but to somehow abolish or at least reduce my unwanted and aged paunch. But could it be done? I read somewhere that getting a six-pack starts in the kitchen. It makes sense. That's where I always got my six-packs from! Anyway, some fitness buffs say that eighty percent of weight loss is a result of proper nutrition and not exercise. Great, now that I had so many more free minutes, I could easily plan my meals, begin dining "properly," and stop the madness of fatness. Ha, ha. I was such an oxymoron, and I thought I was smart. A smart-ass perhaps, but not bright enough to have figured out how to stay slim. Oh, I first sampled most of the pricy, popular, balanced dinners that arrive in boxes by mail, either frozen or fresh. My verdict? Soggy cardboard tastes better, much like the packages that the food came wrapped in. I even branched out to partake in the "psychological" approaches to weight loss (e.g. Noom) and found that being constantly vigilant about what stuff I stuffed into my piehole made me anxious and irritable. Who has the time or mental fortitude to be harangued by a computer algorithm, and then to agonizingly analyze the daily input of calories and from whence they came? Wait a minute, how about me? I'm now retired and have the time for a course correction or for any such mindful foolishness, don't I? Ha, ha. No, I don't! I have also tried and tasted just about everything dietarily available "out there" to not only help me maintain a relatively cis-manly and athletic physique, but to modulate my longstanding battle with chronic Lyme disease. However, nothing has really stuck thus far, and my fat still sticks to me. My longstanding and long-suffering wife doesn't call me Boba Fat for nothing! The old bod might retain some sportiness, but no longer cuts a crisp figure, darn it. Kind of like my 2013, pepper-white, Mini Cooper Roadster; it looks rather snazzy on the outside but has hard miles on it and is not as nimble as it once was. Like me, it tries to be a true "sports" car and perhaps achieves it on rare occasions, but only if pushed hard. Anyway, back to diet and nutrition. Calorie counting, intermittent fasting (Islamic Ramadan does not count), Weight Watchers, SlimFast, NutriSystem, etc. are but a few of the hundreds, if not thousands, of niggardly choices available to tame a burgeoning potbelly and then in turn, to help stave off diseases such as hypertension and diabetes. Do they all work? Probably. But are they all sustainable for long haulers? Probably not. And do they work equally for everyone? Hell no! But the bigger question is: Do restrictive diets coupled with commonsense consumption lower BMI and inflammation and quell longstanding chronic illnesses? Most likely, and there is abundant scientific literature espousing those claims. Losing weight seems to be the single most important factor for achieving overall wellness, period! However, as already stated, I have willingly participated in many such "programs" only to be bitterly disappointed with the outcomes. I know, I know – metabolism, heredity, etc.; it is a complicated topic. Nevertheless, after so much trial and error, mostly error, it appears that utilizing a unique, custom-made nutritional diet, while taking into account a person's genome and body morphology, seems to be the obvious answer to losing unwanted weight. Again, trial and error I'm afraid, because how many budgeted seniors have the fiscal means to get to this high level of customized programming? Very few, if any. So, what can be done? I say to fully embrace diet and nutrition as a lifelong commitment and priority instead of as a casual dalliance whenever the mood strikes. In other words, slow and steady and at a pace and place where a body can be gradually modified. And this decision has to be made Taco Pronto because there is no time to waste. My tummy has a mind of its own and I really mind that it wishes to expand at all costs while my mind wishes the opposite. Instead of uttering Nancy Reagan's eponymous 1986 phrase, "Just Say No," I said YES to health and fitness and started to believe in mind over matter and not to mind if the matter doesn't always cooperate! Anyhow, that dynamic duo of spot-on dieting and nutrition is what we all strive for, no matter the age of the participant.

Unfortunately, it's futile to rely solely on online algorithmic models or on personal fitness fanatics to figure things out for most fatties. It's hard to believe impossibly fit trainers or nutritionists who basically state that, "THEIR past performance does not guarantee YOUR future success;" it is much like stock market investing. Duh! It is up to the individual to determine what works best and then to abide by it, as fervently as if it is a full-time job. Being "trim" is a time-consuming pursuit and does seem to ameliorate chronic sicknesses to a point. I will say that the noble goal of a cellulite-free middle zone has aided me greatly in my quest for overcoming the niggling symptoms of chronic Lyme disease. But the journey has not been easy. My body wants to be a content fatty no matter what. In the end, is it worth it to deny myself a decadent dessert once in a while? I mean, why am I alive if not for a piece of pecan pie at bedtime? Ha, ha. But seriously, if any senior citizen can juggle that kind of unbalanced thinking with a balanced diet and get stellar results, please contact me post haste – I am willing to put down my pale ale and listen! And now, for some anecdotal dietary bullshit that does not always follow the science, much like most of the politically expedient and twisted truths that came out of the mouths of "physician experts" during the Covid crisis. You know, the same "democrat doctors" that gleefully derided the previous administration for its moronic medical miscues but who have now hypocritically capitulated and largely disappeared from the airwaves. Just a quick aside: Before retiring as a lowly, no-account, and APOLITICAL dentist, I exchanged the daily wearing of surgical blue masks for white N95's in January 2020 because even I easily deduced that Covid was a potentially dangerous AIRBORNE illness. Commonsense dictated that a high level of protection from and treatment for the deadly AIRBORNE virus was needed – by using vaccines, antibody treatments, anti-viral drugs, REAL masks, ventilation, physical barriers, etc. Furthermore, if there was a time to panic, that was the time, yet many unwary people did not and died. And a subsequent change in U.S. leadership made no difference and the medical missteps, paltry pablum and putrid punditry continually pour out of Washington. How sad, but utterly predictable! Now, will I continue to wear N95 masks outside the dental office like I have been, in spite of being surrounded by maskless people who think the pandemic is over or never believed it ever existed? You tell me, because I haven't had a single cold or smelled bad breath since January 2020! Of course, I draw upside down smiley faces in black magic marker on the masks to show my displeasure with the nasty virus. Anyway, if all those formerly opinionated TV doctors and media shills could spew such unbelievable, juxtapositional, and politically tainted science, why can't I? Well, here is some more dietary poppycock to digest: My athletic, entomologist daughter keeps her body-fat and overall mass in check by avoiding "useless carbs" and powerlifting. Yes, powerlifting. She metamorphosed from high school tennis and track into Parkour and Crossfit while at college, and eventually to competitive powerlifting. She and her like-minded husband continue their plant and heavy-protein-based eating habits while "lifting" daily and are successfully achieving their mental and physical goals of staying in shipshape. It works for them, but that kind of lifestyle sounds very taxing and "heavy" to me. As an aside, both were formerly nationally ranked powerlifters in their respective, gendered, weight classes. And then there is my athletic, attorney son's ongoing *diet* which, after poking fun at it for over three decades, I may finally embrace and emulate. He was born in Lake Winnipesaukee as part of a litter

of three and he's the one we kept. Wait a minute, that's a paraphrased and stolen line from a favorite Three Stooges episode. I'm so sorry, not so sorry! Anyhow, he was delivered visually disabled (genetic achromatopsia) and developed into a finicky eater, going so far as not liking disparate foods touching each other on his dinnerplate. Besides very poor vision, his total colorblindness made even yummy victuals appear bland and gray. Therefore, he did not trust conglomerated foodstuffs such as lasagna, casseroles, etc., or any tender vittles that appeared to look "complicated" and that he could not readily discern. So, basically, he began life eating in a self-imposed, Spartan way, mindfully chewing through the separated portions of the food pyramid in front of him. As he got older and became a prep school sports star and three-letter man, he went a step farther when strapping on the feed bag or sticking his snout in the trough. He would usually dine three-times-per-day. However,

each sparse (and that may be the crux of it)
meal consisted of only one type of food. For
instance, dairy products for breakfast, meat for
lunch, pasta for dinner and fruits for a snack
(not Fruit Snacks). No more balanced
individual feedings for him. No, when he ate
steak, that was it; when he ate a bowl of egg
pastina with a pat of Kerrygold Irish butter
and a sprinkle of sea salt on top, that's all he
swallowed at that sitting. He explained to me
that it was his intuitive eating principles that
kept him at a sporty buck fifty-five, at five foot
ten. He boastfully claimed that it made sense
and that his digestion never veered off course
due to extraneous calories being dumped all at
once into his stomach. He reasoned, although
unscientifically, that his intestines could then
better process the individual nutrients that
were eaten at separate times without his body
storing redundant glucose as fat. How could I
argue with that kind of lawyerly logic and
bodily success story when he obviously looked

and ate the part, so to speak? Although now with less time for hard-core athletic indulgence, it appears his diet continues to be the lynchpin of his wellbeing and enviable physique. But I'm not jealous and am one proud papa. And you know what "they" say: "Don't reinvent the wheel, just copy it." After due diligence and deliberation, I think I might. However, perhaps I should copy Victoria Beckham's (Posh Spice) twenty-five-year nutritional juggernaut, instead. Besides grueling daily workouts with a super-pricy personal fitness trainer, she reportedly grazes on a calorie-restricted daily menu of grilled fish and boiled vegetables. Nothing more and nothing less. Nevertheless, it sounds awfully boring and possibly a sign of mental instability. Willpower is one thing, but forced dietary deprivation, with a smattering of alleged OCD thrown in is another. But just look at her: middle-aged, gorgeous, and always magazine-cover ready.... And what about periodic fasting, or at least paying homage to that concept? It sounds rather good on paper and there are two valid reasons why it should work: less caloric intake and a long digestive rest between feedings. Consequently, I tried the 5:2 protocol (five days of food and then two days off with only 500 liquid calories on those two starvation days), and almost passed out. I found out the hard way that malnourishment is different than nourishment. I then tried the 8:16 plan (noshing during an eight-hour window and then putting down the spork for sixteen), and no appreciable weight came off my mesomorphic frame. Rats! I had valiantly tried to limit total calories and slowly began to behave like those test-monkeys that zoologists purposefully calorically deprived. I became progressively more irritable (if that's possible) and hard to live with. But animal biologists insist that the research-monkeys live thirty percent longer than their brethren when put on suppressed eating regimens. I don't know; I'd rather be a plump ape than so aggravated and hungry as to throw my feces around the cage, I mean living room. Perhaps pedestrian Veganism is the way to go? However, as I understand it, that diet excludes meat, but can include Oreos, Ho Hos and Drake's Cakes. Wtf? So maybe only downing organic, clean, unprocessed, vegetable matter is what "fundamentalist Vegans" are really talking about? Is that correct? Should I listen to *American Idiot* by Green Day and have a "green" day, every day? I just don't know. But maybe a pescatarian (fish and seafood) diet is the one to follow? However, fish have faces, unlike broccoli and brussel sprouts. But what about clams? Do they have teeny-weeny faces? Is clam chowder "legal"? Man, am I confused. Maybe just munching on fruits and vegetables is the bomb. No meat, no "bad" carbs, no extra sugars, no spices. It didn't work out so well for billionaire Steve Jobs, though. He died of pancreatic cancer regardless of a "recuperative and restorative" sugary-juice and veggie diet that he imposed upon himself in a dying belief that it would save him. The 1970 ELP song *Lucky Man*, written by Greg Lake at age 12, comes to mind. Who says that profound wisdom only comes with advanced age? Nevertheless, there are yet more things to consider: what about drinking less alcohol, trying "Mediterranean," not eating after 6pm, abandoning exogenous sugar and salt, and drinking volumes of expensive water while thinking positive thoughts? And what about Paleo, Keto, Neanderthal, or Roadkill dining? Wow, will all the above-mentioned ploys deliver the results that retired Roly-Polies so desperately seek? I don't know, but latching onto fad after fad with a concomitant messianic zeal each time did nothing for me. Those trying tenures just made me morose and miserable, and more so than usual whenever the bathroom scale numbers initially ticked downward before frustratingly reversing. The yo-yoing was inevitable, or so it seemed. Nothing I had tried as a quick fix was sustainable. Eliminating certain food groups, as suggested by the trendy elimination diet, eliminated everything but my body fat. And the cleanse diet, periodically flushing out "toxins" from either or both ends, is questionable. I never tried it. And one more thing - those sexy, young, fitness instructors that advise intense, sweaty HIIT or TABATA workouts are often bushwhacking seniors as well. You practically have to turn into them full time to possibly get the benefits they preach. So, with precious extra hours on the one hand and a beer in the other, perhaps I should finally seize the day and seriously get in serious shape once and for all. But how? Instead, this old duffer is muddling through retirement complaining and trying like hell to ignore the obvious aging process and the frustrations that accompany it. Yeah, I stay active, crunch "clean" salads while crunching sit-ups, and hit balls with paddles. And on top of that, now I'm mostly "green"; I still love steak, but my heart hates cholesterol! In conclusion, I find that daily motion, be it power walking, running, athletics, etc., coupled with less calories and mostly vegetative consumption may be the best way for me to go. Am I consciously uncoupling from all *bad* food and alcohol? Nah! And am I mindful while dunking my donuts? Hell no! But at least I have a game plan, as tattered and soporific as it sounds. Boring and for the long term, it is for boring losers like me and not for losers who want to instantly lose half of themselves. But so, what. I'm still considered obese based upon my anorexic doctors' wizened opinions. I even try to verbally cajole my darn scale into favoring me. But even THAT inanimate metal object refuses to cooperate. And all this while trying not to think of my stout family tree and its sturdy

Eastern European roots. Maybe that's quite enough vindictive vitriol and I should just be content to waddle through my final years without obsessing about shedding weight; something that I simply am not good at. I'll most likely drop those last and stubborn pounds after death. That will sure show me, won't it?

8

Healthy, Wealthy, and Wise - Or Maybe Just a Wiseass?

Healthy is as healthy does, as Forrest Gump might have said! And I guess wealth accumulation and wisdom might be considered in the same light. The very last word in the above titular phrase applies to all the light-hearted oldsters out there who choose NOT to be overly cynical, judgmental, or terminally aggravated. They appreciate karma, Murphy's Law, and warily understand that retired life is often a tragic comedy. Let's tacitly examine that title's first three facets of anticipated elderly existence, albeit with a bit of snarky repertoire thrown in. Whenever I encounter a svelte senior, I instantly grow fatter, suspicious, and suspect foul play. I have been known to stop and stare as well. Not long enough to provoke a nearby *wokeness warrior* into filing a criminal assault charge against me, but long enough to scrutinize the situation and try to make sense of it. A thin senior citizen? For real? He/she/it must be a geriatric fitness instructor (Jack LaLanne comes to mind), failing cancer patient, marathon runner, porn star, anorexia victim, or homeless hobo. It couldn't be from eating right, exercising, taking Geritol and stool softeners; or could it? What the hell? Perhaps that willowy and wiry specimen of womanhood/manhood/*transhood* was an aberration, a genetic fluke, or a result of successful gastric bypass surgery? I mean, I've seen plenty of high school reunion photos and always marvel at that one statuesque human who stands out like a sharpened pencil amongst a field of couch potatoes. But hold on there, *Phatman*! I am speaking as if burgeoning portliness is unavoidable, cannot be reversed and is something that conventional dieting and exercise can barely touch. Is that true? Medical problems such as elevated A1C scores, pre-metabolic syndrome, hypertension, increased stroke risk, etc. have all been tied to having an excess BOTTOM, one that usually enlarges with age. Unfortunately, it sounds inevitable, to say the least. However, it's not that U.S. citizens (and illegal aliens that will most likely vote democrat) haven't been adequately warned. Americans have been told ad nauseum to lose weight since the '60s, way before they all turned 60, remember? They were also told to put down those unfiltered Camels and jiggers-full of Seagram 7 while simultaneously watching TV commercials extolling smokes and booze. Weight loss is the magic key. And it probably is the ultimate solution for getting rid of chronic inflammation, a main culprit that causes weight gain. It's a vicious cycle that should be killed but, is that realistic? Nonetheless, physical AND mental inflammation from illnesses and stress multiply over the years. Maybe that's why most people blow up and cannot easily purge that poundage, no matter how hard they try. Sure, if modern humans could easily get rid of all accumulated problems and psychological stressors, perhaps they would have a fighting chance in the battle of the bulge. I won't bore you again with all the various diets, supplements, and fitness advice that I have tried over the years to remain in "shape" for competitive sports and sex. It has been TRYING to say the least. I tried to relate my many shortcomings in the previous boring vignette, remember? Anyway, my old body has rebelled and outsmarted me at every turn. Selective fasting slowed down my metabolism and eating small meals throughout the day was a joke. My body also didn't pay any attention to mindful eating. Always having a full mind is difficult to overcome. And daily weigh-ins and calorie counting were scoffed at by my fat cells as exercises in futility. As an old man, I have somehow lost my mind-body connection. My belly behaves like my two cats: They don't listen to me and have brains of their own. And I have come to realize that the "new" intuitive eating mantra and "retro" anti-diet diets are actually the old dietary habits that came naturally to me as a teenager. But not anymore. Okay, I have largely embraced a poor-man's, "Mediterranean" way of eating because it supposedly gets the best long term results. No sugar, no soda, no salt, no nothing. It's basically an elimination diet replacing burgers and hard liquor with nutritionally enriched fiber. My goal was to look like a Greek God, but unfortunately, I still resemble a Goddamn Greek (that's a joke). But for the love of God, please don't make me give up that veggie-brewed, alcoholic concoction called beer. Good golly, I gotta swill my High Gravity brew (Steel Reserve 211)! Anyway, as I age, I find that I am not losing heft, just maintaining it, which is frustrating and demoralizing. Perhaps hereditary is more at play than I realized. My athletic but sturdy parents gave rise to an athletic and sturdy son, and a subsequently athletic and sturdy, gray-haired senior. Will SlimFast cure that? I doubt it. Neither will Slim Jims. Oh boy. Basically, when it comes to dining, moderation is the key, and I will probably take my muscular and slightly flabby love handles to the grave. However, I will be in good company in the cemetery because I have yet to see Vegans, or any such nutritional zealots, outliving the rest of humanity by a wide margin. So, what does it mean to be considered healthy in retirement? Obviously, we cannot and should not do the physical things we used to. And we cannot control genetics or physical and mental maladies as part of "normal" aging. For instance, no one expects menopause or low T, but they magically appear anyway! Maybe the best retirees can do is TRY to achieve lean body morphology. But at the same time, it's often the least thing that can be accomplished. What a dilemma! Speaking of pure exercise, the piddling amount that most people engage in does little to move the scale needle. After the first bunch of pounds melt away due to "metabolic and neurogenic shock," the inevitable plateau hits and the weight tends to stay there. However, if feeling good, maintaining muscle mass and cardiovascular integrity is the goal, then moderate exercise is fine and dandy. But if top to BOTTOM body-shaping is the goal, then we need to really go batty and become either malnourished tramps, supplement-gobbling fitness fanatics or professional athletes. None is likely as we approach the zenith of our lives, hence the inflating BMI's that usually ensue. But unlike expanding waistlines, expanding wealth is both desirable and necessary in our capitalistic system. Medicare and Social Security are fine social safety nets although they alone cannot keep most retirees adequately buoyed to live the perceived "good life". However, legislating additional and generous governmental monetary programs to include the elderly may be an option. Who doesn't want extra "freebie" monthly checks automatically added to their COLA pennies? But most folks also recall what Margaret Thatcher once uttered: "The problem with socialism is that it works until it runs out of other peoples' money." Venezuela, Cuba, and the bankrupt old Soviet Union are a few examples of basically failed states. Nevertheless, I realize that the U.S. can keep printing greenbacks infinitum as long as our legal tender is the world's currency. That fact alone can keep our nation's deficit economy humming along. Keep on printing, baby! National debt and stagflation be damned! Conceivably, the government COULD get more involved and fulfill retirement dreams and desires with substantial increases in Social Security and Medicare benefits. Why not do a *solid* for the seniors? Why not, indeed? However, I haven't seen old people dancing in the streets even in those "model" pseudo-socialistic Scandinavian nations. Thusly, most retirees, regardless of the country, must try to preplan their financial futures as much as humanly possible to avoid the proverbial poorhouse. But like yo-yo dieting and its resultant ups and downs, saving up a worthy nest egg can be problematic for the vast majority of people. Not all of us can be millionaire sports figures or billionaire tech gurus. We also cannot systematically pad our bank accounts by *wheeling and dealing* on Wall Street or be corrupt government public servants that are "entitled" and privy to insider trading information. So, between taxes, rules and regulations that quash only the common man's road to riches, and a fickle stock market that can't be timed, how can most retirees sail off into the sunset on a yacht instead of a leaky dinghy? Just how do measly mice compete with the fat cats for a piece of the American pie? Unfortunately, long-term fiscal planning, sacrifice, perseverance, and patience are required, along with a good bit of luck; accrued financial wisdom may be overrated! It sounds boring and a direct opposite of the new-fangled and seemingly get-rich-quick schemes of potentially suicidal online "Influencers," "YouTubers," and "TikTokkers." "Here today and gone tomorrow, but at least I made a quick buck on hedonistic malarkey and voyeurism," seems to be "their" bleating battle cries while simultaneously dissolving into self-pity and depression. And then most disappear altogether – good riddance. And like hitting the lottery, that's probably not the way to a secure senior retirement. Nevertheless, it is a difficult proposition to position oneself for a soft landing upon retiring. Unlike our federal legislative bigwigs who have golden parachutes with which to land, common Americans will most likely have a hard landing. In addition, wild equity stock fluctuations and intermittent bear markets can wipe out a retirement nest egg in a snap. Then what is left to invest in? Perhaps dabbling in real estate as a fulltime slum landlord or playing the bull market in hopes of being the next day-trader deluxe? Is that the ticket to ride? Wow, my head is spinning. Even supposedly safe havens like mutual funds can tank in a hurry. And as the monetary worries and risks rise, so does blood pressure, stress, bodily inflammation, weight, etc. It's a goddamn shame that wealth and health are so inexorably tied together. No wonder I can't make any headway in the health department! And what about boomerang kids, unexpected health crises, ailing pets, and sick mothers-in-law that wish to move in? Bad stuff happens regardless to the best laid plans. As a result, the anxiety levels and fat cells continually grow while bank accounts recede. But wait, what about selling everything, telling familial and familiar moochers to fuck off, and moving abroad to become a happy, healthy, and wealthy expat? It sounds like a wise plan, doesn't it? But those cheap daydreams can be dashed quickly. Are there great doctors and hospitals abroad? You know, ones that can actually save you? Will the traveling be a nightmare each and every time, or will you go and never come back? Will you regularly invite annoying family and friends that keep your anxiety levels elevated? Will there be kidnappings or a coup d'etat in the new and improved digs? Those are important questions to be answered, regardless of the blabber from countless retirees who have made the move to supposedly greener financial pastures by leaving this great country. I personally know of many who took the ballyhooed plunge, even to the crime-ridden U.S. Virgin Islands, and have quietly come back to be closer to top-notch medical care, doting offspring and familiar food. Or maybe a senior citizen should retire peacefully in the same rural village where she/he was raised, with a solid community of old friends, familiar vistas, restaurants and peace of mind not found on an exotic island in the Caribbean. Ah, the benefits of small town living as we age: money and wellness can be stretched with a frugal, slower pace of life surrounded by reassuring memories. It worked for my wise folks, and it may work for me.

9

Chronicity

Chronicity, not to be mistaken for that 1983, New Wave, Police album called *Synchronicity*, is usually associated with some sort of long-lasting medical malady. A whole panoply of deleterious health conditions fall into this catchall category including Chronic Fatigue Syndrome, Fibromyalgia, RA, MS, etc. Acute illnesses are usually diagnosed and treated appropriately by today's medicine, however, it's the chronic ones which often slip by without easy solutions or therapies. They can malignantly linger for a few months, years, decades or a lifetime. These are the shitty silent killers that don't kill but hang around and make life miserable and unbearable. Sometimes there is a window of respite, of remission, but often the symptoms return. This is not to denigrate the disabled or those who suffer from known chronic ailments like cancer, arthritis, hypertension, asthma and diabetes. What I am talking about are illnesses formerly dismissed as psychosomatic; ones with few visible markers that easily point to a known disease entity or process. Something like Covid long hauler syndrome – a syndrome with many moving parts that science has yet to fully decode, never mind treat. I have personally battled initially misdiagnosed Lyme disease and its subsequent long-term sequelae. The last two decades have been very unpleasant, with a constellation of psychological, muscular, cardiac, and neurological manifestations that spontaneously pop up just when things seem quiet. I have great respect and feel the utmost sympathy and empathy for fellow sufferers of similar diseases. The most troublesome are the ubiquitous autoimmune illnesses that so many people seem to be afflicted with. However, blood tests usually show normal values. And the overlapping psychological effects often obscure and cloud the clueless physician's judgement when deciding on proper therapies. Well-meaning doctors, and even those in it for the money only, are traditionally at a loss when seeing a "zebra patient" amidst a daily deluge of common coughs and colds. Even so-called specialists are commonly flummoxed, as if they were suddenly evaluating old "Doc" Brown's flux capacitor and can't comprehend how it works. Wouldn't it be nice to have a real Dr. House around to "magically" treat the walking wounded, especially the vulnerable elderly? But we are so not there yet. Watching good ole Dr. McCoy on old Star Trek episodes wave his Tricorder this way and that to make accurate diagnoses would be great in our century, too. Perhaps it won't be fictional in the future? I can only wish. Nonetheless, the never-ending online medical threads that I have read, featuring thousands of sick people without a definitive diagnosis and with no hope of a quick cure, are astronomical. It's bad enough to fight constipation, incontinence and memory loss all at once. But couple that with a debilitating illness that has no conventional treatments and growing old really starts to suck! But should senior citizens just take it lying down? Hell no! Now is the time to hit back with the "weapons" currently available, to at least make the most of discomforting lives. Let's begin with what has and has not worked for me over the years in my quixotic quest for well-being while continually being let down by the "medieval" medical profession. I began feeling poorly on May 28, 1994 and suspected that a tick bite was responsible. However, I did not sport the classic bullseye rash indicative of active infection and subsequently received two negative Western Blot tests. I was told emphatically by a medical "expert" that I did not have Lyme disease and to get a psych evaluation ASAP for my symptoms of anxiety, brain fog, bodily rashes, heart palpitations, extreme fatigue, muscle aches, neck neuropathy, disequilibrium, dizzy spells, presyncope, panic attacks and spatial disorientation. Whew! However, and just in case, the doctor loaded me up with thirty or so supplements, in two giant paper shopping bags, to take as directed. Although a former pharmacist, most of them I had never heard of, and they did absolutely nothing for me as I continued my downward spiral. Meanwhile, I visited numerous other physicians to get second, third, and twentieth opinions. All gravely shook their collective heads and said it was all in my head. Finally, out of desperation I put myself on a high dose, six-month regimen of a popular, cheap-ass antibiotic - Amoxicillin. And guess what happened? After barely weathering the initial six months, and after selling my dental practice and temporarily retiring because I could hardly work anymore, I felt myself slowly pulling out

of the nasty nosedive I had been in. And by
1995 I felt almost human again. Almost. And
by May 28, 1996, I was vastly improved. It had
been two years of a dogged struggle, but I
found myself alive and ready to rumble once
more. I restarted a new practice in a nearby
locale and began my professional and home
life anew, with daily receding symptomatology.
I could actually mow my lawn again without
having to come in to rest every five minutes. I
could be in the hot sun once more without
feeling faint. I could finally hit a few tennis
balls and run them down as well, just like I
used to. Hurray! However, that initial
euphoria did not last. Unfortunately, the
lingering side effects of having had Lyme
never completely abated and inconveniently
bother me to this day. There is an abundance
of literature that posits the various scenarios of
having been infected by that damn bacterial
spirochete. No one knows for sure if it is a
persistent uncured infection or permanent

cellular damage that sometimes turns the acute disease into a chronic condition. And, although many of my athletic, physical, and mental powers returned, now I face plain old vanilla aging as an additional burden to add to my slow decline. Anyway, in 2016 I was once again bitten by a tick. But this time a pathognomonic, circular rash appeared, and I ingested Doxycycline 100mg twice daily for two weeks, as per the latest scientific research. The rash departed, and I did not become super-ill like I once was. And, just to make sure, I saw another medical "expert" and had my blood checked with the latest and most specific tests available. Lo and behold, the results indicated that I did indeed have a recent bout of Lyme disease but more importantly, had chronically had it since 1994! Vindication, at last! I knew I wasn't crazy, well perhaps a wee bit.... Nevertheless, in addition to using Amoxicillin, those "lost years" 1994 – 1996 saw me try lots of treatment modalities in hopes of stopping the active phase of my ailment. Some of those same therapies are employed to this day to help me with the nagging aftermath of Lyme. Of course, I had read all there was to read when initially figuring out that I might have Lyme disease (although all my blood tests were negative at the time). I even spoke to a renowned infectious disease physician in the Boston area who concluded over the phone that I most likely had Lyme and needed to get my body as healthy as possible to fight it. The books, online blogs and articles, and the Boston doctor all reiterated that a stark change in eating habits and lifestyle were paramount for my recovery, besides the antibiotic I was taking. Though not magical in any sense and maybe not germane to the host of bizarre maladies affecting other humans, many of the following treatment methodologies that I employed may be applicable to "mysterious and non-mainstream" illnesses. Exercise, rest, and proper nutrition were and have become my three main weapons of choice when confronting Lyme and its ongoing saga. Before 1994 I was a lifelong sporty specimen and tennis was my game. You know, practicing here and there, winning competitive singles tournaments here and there. It was easy staying in shape even though there was regular irregularity in the way I physically pushed my body. But after becoming sick and tired, and initially not being able to pick up a racquet, fitness suddenly took on a whole new meaning. Juggling heavy weights, treadmill work, and calisthenics became my new regimen regardless of how I was feeling. And even though I had lost confidence in my physical and mental abilities I decided to "Suck it up, Buttercup." Many days I wasn't up to it, but this dumbbell descended into the cellar to pick up dumbbells and put them back down, to get on the treadmill, etc. Sometimes my workouts were an hour long, sometimes they lasted five minutes. However, it was determination and perseverance that drove me to keep on truckin.' I was feeling like poop all the time anyway, so why not lift a few barbells? How much worse could I feel? Well, all that physical fitness helped enormously and to this day I manage to squeeze in intense, short workouts to maintain some semblance of weight control and muscle tone. That's in addition to playing sports, as least at some level. I retired from tennis in 2018, basically due to bad knees, recent knee arthroscopies and boredom, mainly the latter. After beating every local and allegedly *male* player in my age group many times over for the last thirty-plus years, one day I stuck my professional, custom-weighted, ProKennex rackets into my tennis bag for the last time and switched over to outdoor pickleball and indoor table tennis, using top-of-the-line Gearbox pickleball paddles and a Killerspin-bladed, Tenergy-rubbered ping pong bat, respectively. And I continue to snowshoe, using the same Dion skids that won me four international gold medals years ago. Hopefully those three activities will not become boring for me. I guess I can always turn to competitive cornhole and use my Ultra-made, Hang Loosey bags that are ready to be "air-mailed" anytime! Of course, being somewhat of a butt nut, I may have gone overboard when applying myself to athletic endeavors and the respective "proper" equipment involved. And don't get me started on the types of javelins that I use when competing in the old-man's division of USATF-sanctioned track and field meets. Actually, I use a 600g Polanik aluminum spear but have been known to chuck a steel Nordic, as well. But that's just me. My obvious advice is to stay very active, even if it involves hot yoga, Orange Theory, speed walking, or tantric sex. Bodily motion assists in all phases of life whether you are an athlete or not; it got me over the hump and the speed bump of my medical misfortune. In addition, it also helps to get motivated by getting kitted out with all the "right" gear. You gotta look good to play well, as I always say, and I continue to push the boundaries of outrageous style when actively engaged in exercise. Rest is the next stop on our wellness journey. And what a bunch of hogwash it can be! How can you get adequate 7-10-hour nightly slumber when in pain, suffering from mental anguish or when not in possession of a MyPillow - pillow? Ha, ha. Anyway, adequate rest or sleep is now highly touted as one of the pillars of wellness and supposedly can help in weight loss/control, forestall memory diminution, increase mental acuity and fight depression. But who has the time for such sleepy shenanigans? "Gulping down a hot pot of fresh Joe after staying up late, barely brushing your choppers and then literally flying out the fuckin' door" was the dominant daily routine for many middle-aged, working folks for years. Now the newly retired are being told the opposite and about how valuable it is to catch those elusive Z's. What? Which commercials should I selectively pay attention to on TV? The somnolence-enhancing mattress advertisements featuring nubile, sexy male and female models that ought to be fucking instead of sleeping, or the Starbucks and Dunkin' Donuts adverts that seek to keep people going against all odds? What a confusing time to live in, especially for the already confused and bewildered gray-caps, like me. Nevertheless, more restful sleep is intuitively beneficial, and even selective napping is deemed therapeutic. There is no need to harp on the subject; extra and profound sleep, enhanced by OTC sleep aids and Ibuprofen if necessary, greatly aided me during my active Lyme ailment and will most likely help others in similar quandaries. To sum up, taking a time out to get some shuteye should no longer be viewed as a waste of time but a legit form of personal health maintenance, although it can be stubbornly evasive – just when retirees need it most! However, besides exercise and sleep there is that "elephant in the room" called diet. As already written about in the previous two vignettes, it has been very difficult for me to maintain any kind of physique with exercise and a stringent diet. Unlike the *Hanged Man* of the Major Arcana in the Tarot cards, many times I would admit defeat and stop the sacrifice. I continually craved rewards for all my deprivation and still do. Unfortunately, that's what gets me in trouble. A little ice cream here and there and the next thing you know, Fatso Fogarty! Even now, as a wizened old wisenheimer, I continually scratch my mostly bald pate and reflect on all the failed attempts I have made throughout life while attempting to restore my bruised dietary ego. Anyway, I will keep on struggling because what have I got to lose except my distended gut? Lol. *And now for something completely different*, as the Monty Python crew once said. Well, actually more of the same but along slightly different lines. Legal and illegal supplements as bona fide therapeutics for maladies such as menopause, Low T, E.D., hair loss and aging exploded years ago and continue to cloud legitimate medical therapies with rational-sounding rejoinders and nouns. Are vitamins, nootropics, functional-organics, biologicals, pharma-nutrients, phytochemicals, bioflavonoids, antioxidants, organic-analeptics, adaptogens, nutraceuticals, "eleven herbs and spices" and hypochondriacs really the elixirs of continuous youth? And are they also the missing links in aiding chronically ailing people? More importantly, are most of those words real?! Anyway, could some of them benefit me with my ongoing medical disability? Or are they just part of the wellness word salad of a largely unregulated business hoping to snag desperately sick suckers with deep pockets? Now, I'm not disparaging the entire industry, but one could become seriously ill by voluntarily consuming vast quantities of often unproven and nebulous chemical concoctions in the name of "good health." Conversely, if one chronically only takes a few supplements, will they in turn dampen the chronic ailment that they are taken for? Or is that in theory only? Now that's a billion-dollar question! Nonetheless, many chemical compounds such as baby aspirin and vitamins C and D unquestionably squelch weight gain and unwellness due to mitigating (there's that word again) bodily inflammation. And they most likely are logical agents in combating some of the ill effects of long-term disease, as well. But what of supercharged multivitamins, Lipoic acid, glutamine paste, stevia liquid, ashwagandha root, CBD oil, rhodiola root, turmeric, Kava, ginseng, green tea, etc.? Oh my gosh, I can't even begin to list all the foreign sounding but supposedly safe substances that I have ingested or been recommended, not only to fight Lyme disease, but to knowingly keep up with the science Joneses. More FOMO for this FOP, you know. However, do some of them actually work as directed or are the doses so small as to make little difference? And does a placebo effect take over where pharmacological therapies fall short? I don't know and probably no one else does either. But isn't that what senior living is all about? Who will outlive whom and who is constantly caffeinated? Ha, ha, "I take more supplements than you, therefore I must be healthier." Is that GNC's missive and does it aptly apply to all senior retirees, even the severely over-medicated and medically compromised? And what of the many A-hole-istic naturopaths which I visited during my flailing and failing early Lyme sojourn who "prescribed" adrenal-fatigue fighting and thymus boosting concoctions? What the fuck? Not to mention the various homeopathic preparations that were strongly suggested that as a pharmacist, I vehemently disagreed with. The female voodoo witch doctor out in the Appalachian sticks which I once consulted advised eating lots of raw jalapeno peppers as a cure-all tonic for whatever was bothering me. I mean, I was desperate in 1994; I was willing to try any and all supplements, therapies, practitioners and quacks to get well again. However, in hindsight, perhaps some of them DID have an influence on my overall improvement. I recall taking the small victories in stride and keeping the push for a full recovery. Alas, I got to a certain degree of wellness and then plateaued. Anyway, before finally retiring for good I was able to regain most of my former faculties and could drill teeth, work out and play age-related sports at REASONABLY high levels again. And I continue my rigorous and deliberate approach when it comes to eating, exercising, and sleeping. Today, I take only a handful of exogenous, supplemental agents, like baby aspirin, taurate magnesium, CoQ-10, and vitamins C and D. And I APPEAR to have reached a steady state of physical and mindful health. Not a steady state of mind, mind you, but at least my butt is not enlarging. Winning!

10

The Borg

With my tennis history, one might conclude that I have a residual fascination with that stoic Swede Bjorn Borg. Not really - at no time was I ever a fan. I never warmed up to him or his trailblazing usage of exaggerated ping pong strokes on a tennis court, which unfortunately today's top players exclusively use. The Borg I am referring to is from Star Trek: The Next Generation TV series; that science fiction flotsam featuring mostly inane "moralistic" storylines marred by pretentious, overacting actors. However, the episodes involving the Borg, an advanced, communistic civilization of humanoid/robotic lifeforms which sought to assimilate as many other sentient species as possible, reminds me of where modern medicine may be headed. It used to be hearing and visual aids, then cochlear inserts, pacemakers, organ transplants, and face lifts, and then insulin pumps and titanium-based tooth and joint replacements. And now we are knocking on the door of combining gene therapy and stem cells with nanotechnology to truly become Terminator-like beings. It's all good though, if the technology extends our lives and the liberty to pursue happiness. Ah, liberty... that's a whole different kind of science fiction. My dad used to sarcastically enunciate a borrowed line that the Borg may have liked: "You're only free to do as you're told." Anyway, let's back up a bit to examine what's medically and realistically possible today. I have many friends and frenemies who have been "rebuilt," much like the Six-Million-Dollar-Man. Besides prosthetic dental implants and hip or knee replacements, not to mention penile, breast, and lip augmentations, today's humans can sort of limp into retirement with their bodies sort of working and sort of intact. It's the best we have thus far, and it seems to be working giving worn out geezers a second chance at so-called healthy wellness. However, we're not quite at the universally available and biologically viable "implanting mental chips" phase. But I'm sure artificial intelligence wonks are busy plotting a *better* world for young and old alike. And it may very well work out. Psychologically living out pleasant lives in an alternate avatar universe could be just around the corner. And, why not? We already have it, although currently somewhat primitive, in today's gaming, porn, and other addictive online programs. And what with more elderly people already beholden to mechanical and foreign bodily parts and pieces, why not completely replace or enhance the senile mind as well? Chip me! Remember, resistance is futile. Is that a slogan from the Borg collective or from a certain large communist country bordering the Pacific rim? Or both? I'm sorry, but I'm old and cranky and say things that may be misconstrued as politically incorrect. Perhaps as a terminally tired retiree I don't need so much as a new limb or brain as to be reprogrammed at a far east re-education camp. *Oops!... I did it again.* Sorry, but thanks for that line, Britney!

11

Dating and Mating

So much to opine about, and here we go. Has innermost, biologically driven human behavior actually changed in the short amount of time Homos have been on earth? Or even since the sexually adventurous sixties and decadent seventies? Probably not. Most people just want to meet, greet, date, and possibly mate, regardless of where they fall on the sexuality spectrum. Granted, today's worldwide and civilized populace is technically "smarter," empathetic, and seemingly more inclusive than it once was. But why does "society" writ large allow the proverbial pendulum to keep swinging to extremes? Just like the idiotic "new math" that kept periodically popping up in grammar school to great consternation, the current LGBTQ+ militancy of debunking the majority of human nature and legitimizing hitherto minority aberrant and abhorrent behavior should make one pause and think, at least for a moment. First it was the battle of the sexes in the '70s, now it is the "reinventing" of the sexes. Have humans rapidly evolved, become newly enlightened, or is everyone tiredly tolerant? Socrates, Plato, and even my conservative old man harped about the imminent degradation and downfall of mankind due to undue debauchery and the resultant relaxation of unwritten societal mores. But we are still here, cutting off and adding erogenous parts as needed, and building new bathrooms to accommodate the confused and ostracized. I guess you could say that the "modern" online phenomenon in all matters has helped push the envelope, and my buttons, of the acceptance of many things. Horny trolls hiding in their parents' basements and "brainless" influencers espouse numerous erratic and erotic views, some even masquerading as mainstream. And this leads me to some observations about traditional male and female comingling, if you know what I mean. Paleolithic cavemen and cavewomen probably did not have to think too hard when it came to relationships. "Me Tarzan, you Jane" was most likely all that was grunted before the dirty deed took place. Most archaic males and females were lucky enough to be fertile at the same time and to find one another at all. The paucity of available humans made it easier to scratch that primordial itch without the burden of first analyzing sexual preferences. You saw, you fucked, and asked questions later. And if perchance you did not reproduce, your DNA died with you, period. Nevertheless, in today's swiping world, with tantalizing players such as Tindler, Stupid Cupid, Bumbler, Grindr, etc., have we easily solved the mating game once and for all? And for all ages and sexual preferences? And are today's "liberated" heterosexual women eager to mount aboard and do the reverse cowgirl at first meeting with a live male stud? "You've come a long way, baby!" wasn't just a throwaway line for Virginia Slims cigarettes, was it? It meant something, or did it? Oops, I forgot about Time's Up and the #MeToo movements. Duh! And what about STDs that have somehow managed to keep up with mature monkeyshines? Sure, they can be beaten back with medications and protection, but they are still around and ready to stimy romantic interludes in an instant. In addition, horny women appear to want sex on their terms and sometimes those terms are ambiguous at best. Troubled comedian Andy Dick once famously said that "bad dating technique" was the major problem men faced when pursuing unwilling women. And that alone led to misunderstandings and arrests, mainly his. A former disgraced and fallen governor claimed that his ethnic, innocent and flirtatious advances were misconstrued as felonious misconduct. How confusing. Yes means yes, but make sure both inebriated and stoned parties have GoPro cameras strapped to their heads and a jointly signed affidavit before going to bed, right? However, women are the ultimate physical and emotional gatekeepers of sex with the most to lose. It makes sense, but the list of "aggrieved Weinsteins" keeps growing with more and more men being sexually accused, punitively punished, and societally canceled, some due to flimsy allegations alone. Is that also fair? No one is condoning verified rape or sexual assault, but has our "explicit" culture gone too far in both a puritanical and pornographic direction and frustrated the hell out of a lot of "good" people in the middle? That damn pendulum seems to have two bobs and swings both ways at once! And don't forget the promiscuous femme fatales like Madonna, Cher, Ghislaine, and Miley. What message do they send? They appear to come across as provocative, wonton, female predators and only further muddle the distressed dialogue. What sexual rubric do they fit in? And does anything go with them or is it just a tired, phony, dog-and-pony show to keep the money coming in? Sex sells and they might as well be up front and legitimate about it. Why not? If you have tits and teeth, flaunt them and then complain later when things get too real or go awry. After all, it's the American judicial way. As I see it (although I have been nearsighted since birth), most men just want to be men, whatever that is. But can they and should they be? Perhaps it's just too late because I hear lots of grumbling from the "fair" sex. More and more women are complaining, namely saying, "Where are all the good men at?" Really? "Manly" men have been effectively emasculated, demonized, degraded, and portrayed as toxically masculine, non-essential, and obsolete brutes. Feminist icon Irina Dunn once gleefully chortled that "a woman needs a man like a fish needs a bicycle." Maybe she has a point. However, "you reap what you sow," and there seems to be a lot less orgasmic sowing going on. Nowadays, a hard man is indeed good to find! Unfortunately, it's now a flaccid meat market out there for the heterosexual ladies. And there you go. But enough of this seemingly chauvinistic and misogynistic rant. "Nobody loves women more than I!" Did a recent former president really say that? Anyway, it is true for me, as well! I love cis-het women, especially my long-suffering, stoic, and tolerant wife – Hottie Blondie. And to this day I make a virile point of wearing skintight Speedo jammers when on the beach, just to titillate her. No "dad shorts" or Chubbies for me, ever! Hottie Blondie doesn't seem to mind. After all, she's the one who bought them for me to show off my package, for her pleasure I presume. Hey, now! Nevertheless, there are no easy answers or solutions to solve the ongoing mating minefield between allegedly consenting adults, regardless of their chromosomal, biologic origins. But after being so longwinded and dogmatic, unfortunately I have no real tips for my fellow "straight" retirees. Except that sexual wants and needs have no expiration dates, and the "act" can be frustrating to accomplish for the retired and tired set. The haunting refrain from the Talking Heads song *Once in a Lifetime* sums it up succinctly: "It's the same as it ever was," although with less energy emanating from the elderly sexual combatants. The tried-and-true bar scene may be dead but E-disharmony, Matchless.com and Unhinged are alive and well, looking for lying suckers to partake in them, to find that elusive mate and then be disappointed. It's the same as it ever was, but with a cellphone in hand instead of a glass tumbler full of Old Grand Dad. Thank you so much for putting up with my parting shots at humanity's sexuality and my old-school hang-ups. After all, I'm a doddering, cis-gender, old-fashioned, old coot, remember?

12

Senseless

Some people say that I am progressively getting hard of hearing and seeing, but I say it is "hard of learning" that troubles me most. Ha! Anyway, most elderly senses take an unabashed thrashing with time. Some abdicate altogether, although there are numerous aids available to at least shore up the shortcomings of seeing and listening. For the others, including taste, smell, and touch, not so much. *Senseless in Seattle* would be a fantastic avant-garde film noir for retirees, however, who would pay to see or hear (if they could) such sad storytelling? No one, not even nursing home patients, many of whom have one foot in the grave and the other on a banana peel. But the realities of aging can be stark and unforgiving, whereby the visual and auditory perceptions of surroundings are gradually lost due to diminished sensory input. Slowly becoming blind as a bat and deaf as a doorpost are not fun events to look forward to. But wait, what about the other senses becoming stronger to compensate for failing eyesight and hearing? Is that really a thing? I don't know. I do know that I wouldn't want to visit a visually impaired dentist. You know, one who felt around until finding the mouth and then asking the patient for further directions to the offending tooth. And licking or sniffing in the dental operatory would definitely violate the strict rules of OSHA, HIPAA, PETA, #MeToo, Time's Up, Time's In, Time Out, etc. Holy hell, good thing modern medicine has come up with not only glasses, but a slew of surgeries ranging from glaucoma treatments to futuristic genomic dicing and splicing, all to preserve or correct imperfect eyes. A grizzled old goat (NOT greatest of all time) like me could still find my way around molars and bicuspids if by some fucked-up happenstance I was forced back to work. A big thank you is long overdue to my optometrist (Dr. M.) and ophthalmologist (Dr. S.). Dr. M. gives me a yearly vision tune-up and Dr. S. did my Lasik corrective surgery in 2004, which is still working. In addition, hearing aids, cochlear implants, and inner-ear surgeries have greatly aided the hearing impaired to regain lost auditory function. Nevertheless, taste, smell, and touch, although important to humans on an emotional and practical level, cannot easily or readily be restored once lost, such as from a stroke. Taste is one of those tricky senses that is inexorably linked to olfaction. It is a combo affair. Unfortunately, humanoids only have vestigial remnants of super sensitive Jacobson's organ, which is found buried deep in the nasal sinuses. However, it is pronounced in and used by many animals, especially lowly reptiles and amphibians. They use it to great effect to detect a wide range of odors that humans can't. For instance, most snakes use theirs to sense the surrounding environment and when hunting for prey. The endlessly flicking forked tongues pick up volatile molecules in the atmosphere which are then deposited onto the palatal Jacobson's organ inside their mouths. Unlike serpents, most people cannot "taste" the air with their tongues. In addition, the Covid crisis highlighted the loss of smell in some patients and the great length of time that it takes to regain it. But Smell-O-Vision is not coming back any time soon to theaters, so senior citizens can relax and not worry about missing out on any manufactured *stank* when viewing a flick. Anyhow, most retirees are ready to do battle with known foes such as unjust tax audits, tardy garbage collectors, hapless village idiots and wasted Walmart employees, but are often unprepared to lose sights and sounds, besides their marbles. Sometimes those two senses can be rectified and sometimes not. It can be extremely challenging to grow old with dignity while keeping the five senses intact. Nothing says old timer faster than farting in public and then asking "what?" over and over again when questioned.

13

The Feet and Defeat

Corns, bunions, and blisters, oh my. Holy hammertoe, Batman! There are a plethora of afflictions, diseases, injuries, malformations, disorders, and fetishes that involve our most distant appendages and their protruding, nailed, ten digits. Like dentistry and proctology, the field of podiatry is a necessary evil yet is often a stigmatized, maligned, and misunderstood medical profession. I mean, who wants to treat gnarly ingrown toenails and gaze at ugly-looking feet all day? Not I, and I have unfortunately seen many awful-looking mouths in my time. Anyway, everything that biologically gets used continually takes a severe beating, including teeth and footsies. However, healthy feet are linked to independence, mobility and longevity, and hence need to be kept in tip-toe shape. But my God, does Dr. Scholl have to practically move into every household that boasts an AARP subscription? Maybe so. During my years of competitive athletics, no other body parts consistently suffered more than my feet. Sprained and rolled-over ankles, blisters by the bunch, torn toenails, recurrent plantar fasciitis, painful plantar warts, heel bone bruises, multiple metatarsal fractures, compartment syndrome, etc. Whew. And that's when I was young and could patiently and cavalierly limp things off. Nowadays a doctor's visit is mandatory to at least get that gouty arthritis checked out. And maybe to sand down those bothersome, heel callouses, ones that obesity prevents some peeps from reaching anymore. Just one more quick storyline: My tough, old mom began suffering from a painful fourth toe on her left foot and she didn't know what to do. It was a gradual and insidious malady and not a result of sudden injury. However, Epsom salts soaks, massages, and essential oil remedies proved fruitless. But after three general physician's visits, nothing had changed; and then a specialist podiatrist became involved. However, after two painful surgeries, not only to ablate the troublesome nerves and restructure the interior toe phalanges, the excruciating discomfort returned. Meanwhile, I scoured Amazon for the most comfortable track shoes that money could buy so Mom could stride in a straight line without wobbling and wincing. I bought her a few pairs of ultralight cushioned skips, and she was very grateful. She could now stand in pillowy comfort, but it was still uncomfortable for her to walk. More consulting visits to orthopedic medical experts followed, all on account of that darned toe! But nothing further was proposed, and the prognosis was deemed guarded and dire. Case closed. Or was it? Today she regularly power-walks around the college outdoor track year 'round and her "naughty toe" is no longer an issue. Is it mind over matter? Does it still hurt? Or did she refuse to let her feet defeat her? I don't know; she suddenly stopped complaining. But at least she is wearing the thick, soft-soled shoes I bought her. And she has a few spare pairs of additional kicks to go through if she lives that long. I hate feet and I'm sure mine hate me back for all the abuse I continually put them through, even as an aging pseudo-athlete. But that's enough *kvetching* from this hobbling hobgoblin.

14

Retirement, Travel, and Family

I know that my cynical, sarcastic, snarky, and suspicious nature grates on most people. Hopefully my off-balance and quirky attempts at humor tug at their funny bones as well. Case in point: whenever a politician of any age suddenly wants to bow out of a contested race or "retire" from politics, the standard line uttered to the gullible hoi polloi and lame media is that he/she merely wishes to travel and to spend more time with his/her family. Come on. Is that for real? That's funny! And is that what really ends up happening? Not usually. I'm sure many potential "scandals" have been averted by unscrupulous leaders simply by taking the high road called resignation-retirement. "The masses are asses, and they will never find out" is a common refrain of the high and mighty, be they kings, queens, Nixon, or Cuomo. "I'm out now, so leave me the fuck alone" then becomes the obvious mantra of the recently recused. Of course, later we often learn that there was much more to the stories of their hasty departures. The officials resigned not to spend more time with their respective wives, or to visit relatives in Albuquerque more frequently, but to scuttle and squelch any remaining or brewing misconduct. Sometimes we find out about those disgraceful misdeeds and sometimes we don't. However, there is some truth about having more time after throwing in the work towel at a certain chronological age. I mean, the RV business is booming because of the baby boomers. Royal Caribbean boats are stuffed with thousands of fat retirees itching from sunburns while stuffing themselves at the bountiful buffets. And then they roll out to get still more sun on the pooped deck. And major holidays see an uptick of the elderly flying around the world to see Paris sites and to get an eyeful of the Eiffel Tower. So, the evidence is clear that oldsters do indeed travel more and are usually accompanied by significant others and/or children. And, they usually have a few disposable bucks and can afford these expensive junkets. However, can all retirees partake in this permanently relaxed lifestyle? And at what age does it begin, if at all? So, besides traveling, am I spending more time with the old gal and "seeing more" of her now that we are officially retired? Yes and no. The Wuhan-inspired pandemic severely put a crimp in us psychologically. Although vaccinated and boosted, the constant underlying apprehension of courting death at any time was a sexual and vacation-planning buzzkill. Nothing thwarts an erection or a trip faster than unrelenting anxiety. And with capricious lockdowns occurring in many countries, it became foolhardy to go against the grain and purposely travel with a messianic fervor as if your life depended on it. And it may have! Anyway, as long as there is some good health and "working parts" involved, most senior partners should be able to enjoy their extra time together. Unless of course the new dynamic upsets the apple cart and the renewed familiarity breeds contempt instead of love. Oh well, a retired heterosexual couple can always watch a National Geographic TV special about Angkor Wat, dream about going abroad, and hope that the China virus has finally petered out. In the near future, hopefully all can partake once more in domestic and global travel, unless Russia tinkers with a nuclear confrontation. It's always something.

15

"I'm Bored With It All."

And there they are: Winston Churchill's supposedly famous last words; a prophetic phrase also embodied by many retirees, sometimes even before retirement! We've all heard variations of those saliant syllables while growing up and then growing old. But is that the ultimate cop-out or are there sound and sobering arguments behind the alleged boredom afflicting senior citizens? Infamous psychedelic relic Timothy Leary once preached that *cool* young people should "turn on, tune in, drop out." Likewise, should *cooled* elderly "turn off, tune out, and drop off the face of the earth?" Has the looming obsolescence of my generation also taken an accelerated tack due to ageist tomes? It certainly sounds that way. Let's hope there is some pushback, some piss and vinegar left over in collective tired bones to keep on fighting and living. However, there are multiple "valid" reasons for ending up in the discombobulated and tortoise-like lane of life, bored with it all. Let's first examine the words depression and acceptance, and the resultant boring capitulation that often follows. How can a senior citizen remain happy and content if he/she is constantly swimming against the current and not getting anywhere? In fact, sometimes it seems as though the retirement riptide is pulling people farther and farther from shore. Not to despair though, perhaps there is nothing that can be done to stop the presses and just persevering is a noble victory. Perhaps as the Tao states humans, like grass, should bend and not break when the wind blows over them and then can live to fight another day. If we accept our lots in heavy undercurrents, maybe we can successfully swim to safety with dignity and grace. That doesn't sound boring to me. Nevertheless, poor or failing mental/

physical health often puts an additional damper on the best laid plans, no matter the verbal cajoling of mindful gurus such as Dyer or Tolle. Because if you are sick and tired, and tired of being sick, that's a tough row to hoe! How can one keep going when her/his *get up and go musta got up and went* (thank you, Aerosmith)? But perhaps it is also garden variety fatigue and apathy that creep up on old creeps and hinder the joys of living. "Been there, done that" is a favorite saying of my octogenarian mother-in-law. But should life's events be a continual bucket list with boxes to check off and then stop living? Is that what Churchill meant and did? He checked off the Nazis, had one last drink of his beloved sherry, and then checked out due to unrelenting boredom? Possibly. To that end, I am fond of telling my wife about my current and slightly demented mental state. Although often considered to be a funny guy, there is a big difference between the words funny and fun! I tell her that if a limousine were to suddenly pull up in front of our house packed with scantily clad female revelers beckoning me inside with promises of free drinks and sex, and with plans for bar hopping all night and at no cost to me but my time, I would not go. And let's say that miraculously my wife encouraged me to embark on such an erotic outing and tried to push me out the freakin' door? I still would not go. Am I really bored of exposed tits and ass? Say it ain't so. What's wrong with me? I think I still have it, somewhere. In reality, my inherent anxieties, tiredness, and lack of confidence would all contribute to canceling such freebie frivolity. Like those spot-on Progressive commercials about not turning into your parents, I also suffer from a similar syndrome: too many questions, too many insecurities, too many inane rebuttals about having a good time, and, no condoms. Yesteryear saw me willingly endure discomfort, hunger, and angst to get laid or to meet friends at a distant bar and mix it up. It was devastating to miss Mixers or even one Thursday night at my favorite watering hole back in college. Now it blissfully seems boringly natural to stay home on most evenings. I guess comfort and ease trump any monkeyshines that could possibly titillate me. I will add that I mostly speak for myself, and others may vociferously disagree. Many people of means, such as rock stars, politicians and staple tabloid trash appear to be in a constant state of euphoric ecstasy regardless of age or level of infirmity. How many big, fat, fucks have you heard of that seem to defy aging, gravity, and impotence? Tons, and I won't name names. You know who they are. So, is it loads of money, cocaine, and plastic surgery that can prop up rich retirees and give them a sense of renewed youth and vitality, and to periodically upgrade their rides and spouses as needed? Bling, booze, and a new broad to shake off the dullard doldrums? Is that what really conquers boredom? Is that the bottom line? Is money the rate-limiting step as usual? Wow. Nevertheless, I have heard it works for some people. But, mercy me, starting over every few years, regardless of wealth, and ending up with the same old shit down the road doesn't sound like a sound solution. Anyhow, perhaps it's my unique reactionary and sedentary ways of thinking which are contributing to the problem. Besides traveling to our favorite beaches maybe my wife and I should make a concerted effort to get out more to meet and greet, but to what end? I expect we would run into a world we are no longer familiar with and bump into persons that would be toxic to our wellbeing. And you can't swipe left to get rid of the assholes in front of you. Meet and creep would be the new axiom! Anyway, thus far we have covered acceptance, generalized malaise, guilt and lack of enthusiasm as pretexts for not letting go and living it up. Getting stuck in a comfortable rut without a change of scenery probably greatly contributes to that lackadaisical same ole, same ole. But what about suffering from genuinely bad health? Now that can be a real killjoy! What if each day is filled with pain, suffering and just more of the same stressful bullshit that you can't do anything about? You've "accepted," are not depressed, but it still hurts. Is that anything to look forward to, day after shitty day? So, what are some real solutions to keeping retirees moving and shaking regardless of medical disturbances and mental diminution? Reading more self-help books? Or trying to live the virtuous life by eating, drinking, exercising, and sleeping right? Holy moly, that's what got retirees so bored in the first place! What about euthanasia? And not "youth in Asia," as Roseanne Roseannadanna (Gilda Radner of SNL fame) would have said. Why not end the party early if a senior citizen is medically terminal or justifiably, terminally bored? I guess that could be an answer, but it seems a bit harsh to me. There is no digging back out from such a decision and it may not work out for everyone. Anti-depressant medicaments and psychological talks are the standard treatment options when people of all ages fall into a downward, spiraling funk. Retirees are most vulnerable, what with bills and taxes still to pay and the unchecked and relentless anxieties of "living" still in play. Back in the day, slugs of beer or Jim Beam bourbon while yacking with close buddies supplanted pills and cognitive behavioral therapy. You regularly got drunk among your wasted friends and realized that everyone had "situations" going on and not to panic. It was a brotherhood and sisterhood of depressed people, only many didn't know it at the time. People imbibed, inhaled, commiserated, solved each other's problems at least for the moment, and kept on living in a hazy stupor. However, with the advent of SSRIs and other such drugs, now everyone can regain positive mental faculties in a healthful way. Really? Impotence for men, loss of libido for women, and a host of other side effects have unfortunately put a stain on this class of drugs and treatment modality. Of course, some recent medical literature has suggested that SSRIs really work by inhibiting inflammation, which in turn may be a root cause of depression and weight gain. Who knows, perhaps popping a few daily Advil Liqui-Gels might be a simple solution for quelling troubled gray matter and halting that wayward waistline? I know from personal experience that when I take Ibuprofen tablets for aches and pains, I also feel better mentally. Hmmm. Besides the legal drugs and psychobabble prescribed by well-meaning *shrinks*, another highly touted and written-about answer relating to the boring frustrations of humans is GRATITUDE. But is it really the easy panacea we have all been looking for? I don't know, but there are numerous books about it claiming incredible and mind-altering possibilities. It seems that no matter what current state of knackered dilapidation a person is in, just being grateful for waking up in the morning should be good enough to carry one through a lousy day. But is this kind of rosy and delusional positivity even healthy? Is setting the bar of life very low the ultimate source of joy? Should I exalt out loud after putting on my socks or tucking my shirt in? Should I rejoice after defecating, and properly wiping? False flag positivity is annoying when we witness it in other people. So why should we partake in it ourselves? Again, I don't know. Daily positive affirmations smack of arrogant denial and a lack of common sense. Merely *stayin' alive* (thank you, Bee Gees) seems like a moral, but hollow victory. Anyhow, this mopey dope can't change life by staring at the mirror in hopes of gratefully seeing a younger reflection of himself. Evolution doesn't work in reverse.

That once manly image is long gone and it's time to snap out of it. Enough of my complaining and excuses. I say take a few uncomfortable risks as often as possible, even if it means not knowing ahead of time if there will be an available toilet where you are headed. Grit your false teeth while anxiously waiting in a long line at airport terminals because this is your last chance to forestall dying, although maybe not boredom and anxiety per se. Fly to a faraway beach. Why not? Beat back apathy by traveling north to Canada, eh, or south to eat boiled peanuts and Moon Pies. Why not? You only die once, so.... The old lady and I make a concerted effort to shake ourselves out of our static sluggishness and regularly visit our beloved two foreign countries, no matter the distance or the discomforts of the treks. Nervousness and depression be damned. Swimming and sunbathing on warm beaches, cracked-conch sandwiches, and fricasseed octopus go a long way in keeping our otherwise boring lifestyles at bay. For those wishing closer venues such as camping or getting away to anyplace south of the Mason-Dixon line, the trips may be beneficial as well. My wife often forces me to "relax and recharge," and I am always grateful she does. The change of scenery may not vanquish all the accumulated and compounded problems of retirement, however, even baby steps involving hedonistic attempts at pleasure can be rejuvenating. Hopefully most retirees are not too tired or financially strapped to enjoy a few "blasts" of life now and again! And when you return home, keep the feel-good feeling going. Find, unpack, and lace up your platform dancing shoes from the '70s. Then close the curtains, plug in your ancient Technics or JVC turntable, and put on Silver Convention's second studio album. And when the 1976 hit song *Get Up and Boogie* comes on, get up and boogie! That's right!

16

Keeping Up With Cancel Culture

Saying you are non-racist or supportive of the po-po is now considered racist rhetoric! Who knew? How did that happen, along with the profusion of words and sayings that are now off-limits to utter? I can't keep the hell up. Can I even talk anymore without violating someone's principles or piece of mind? What about my own? And what about most comedians and their frequently caustic *shticks*? What should they say, or not say? I just don't know. And I thought getting old and gray meant being revered by the clueless younger generations. Ha, ha! Instead, *they* want me to shut the fuck up. Wowsers! Boy, do I feel old, dumb and suddenly out of touch. But perhaps I should stop grousing altogether because I really don't know what I'm talking about anymore. Or do I? I read the local newspaper daily and dubiously watch both CNN and Fox News for their opinionated and contradictory, national and world views. Not news, but views. And yet I still feel like I am out of the "progressive" loop these days. Back in the '70s, with my long, black, greasy hair and polyester bellbottoms, I felt a kinship to the left-leaning, "domestic terrorists and feminists" who sought to break the conservative stranglehold on government and social constructs, as well as to usher in a benevolent, equal, non-violent, Age of Aquarius. It felt good being part of a "movement" to finally set things righteously right. What went wrong? Plenty. Besides the silly drug use, the pervasive naïveté and hypocritical dogma even back then was palpable. However, socialistic and virtuous inclinations have once again come full circle. But at least the long gone, long-haired hippies could say their piece while flashing the peace sign; now just ONE out-of-context finger salute, or a joking refrain, can get you permanently banned from the online universe, fired from work and banished by friends and family. Holy moly! Today's elite cancel culture kooks have run amok and seem to have hijacked most media and higher thinking. Changing names of high schools, creating safe zones against right-leaning people, removing "offensive" statues, acceptance of sexual deviancies, "correct" pronoun usage, and nebulous virtue signaling have eclipsed ugly world affairs and real domestic problems. But is that really the case? Perhaps, but maybe it is also high time to take a hard look at ourselves, no matter the age, and begin to solve the many accumulated injustices and inequalities all around us. But I don't want to be a social justice warrior and fire-bomb tax-paying businesses under the misguided guise of peacefully protesting and exercising my first amendment rights. Or to freely use "free speech" that is convenient truth for some, but inconvenient slander to others, depending on who is in power. I don't wish to fight for more political correctness or to excoriate nebulous root causes or root for "socialism for thee but not for me." I can't be a latter-day, wide-eyed and willful wokester; I wasn't even a hip hipster, first! I just want to remember all the lingo associated with today's subculture so I can blend in more and not be instantly ostracized, that's all. I gave up saying *cool, far out*, and *groovy* and have embraced modern acronyms to keep up and NOT be canceled. Out with PETA, ASPCA, HIPAA, OPEC, and OSHA and in with GLAAD, LBGTQ+, ISO, FOMO, and MILF. I gotta get it together and rejoin today's jargon-laden society or it will be goodbyes-ville for me. As a post-modern, faux-feminist, I've also come a long way, baby! I'm trying, I really am, and hopefully will continue to fit in although I am biologically a pissed-off, crusty and crinkly, retired, old *man*. And I sort of promise to

keep most of my present and future opinions
to myself as I patiently wait for the proverbial
pendulum to swing back, to restore to a restive
populace a sense of democratic civility and
commonsense. Let's hope I have some time
left to enjoy a braver new world in the future.

17

Productivity, Hobbies, and Distractions

Most people are usually proactive and productive during youth and middle age and have precious little time for recreation. Then they wholeheartedly and mindlessly embrace hobbies and distractions when physically and psychologically infirm. But is this the way things should be? Is this the natural order of life as humans progressively become youth-challenged and cannot work anymore? But can it be effectively changed or mitigated (I love that ostentatious Dr. Fauci-inspired word)? Early medical and mental interdiction may help keep elderly bodies and brains vital, within reason, and subvert the inevitable decline. But is that necessary, just so oldsters can keep slaving away at mindless jobs and postpone Social Security? You know, the senior safety net that the federal government hopes retirees never tap into? I cannot answer those kinds of fiscal or philosophical questions. Anyway, countless songs and their musical earworm effects have reinforced our working lives over the years. Most retired folks still remember inspiring lyrics and melodies from decades ago. There is music denoting anything and everything, including "work." Some of these pieces, such as *Manic Monday* (written by Prince and sung by the Bangles), *Working 9-5* (Dolly Parton), and *Taking Care of Business* (Randy Bachmann) have become classic touchstones reflective of old-fashioned American culture and values. Unlike the most recent "lost" generation of self-entitled, bone-idle, and work-shy millennials, most older people can vividly recall lives where jobs were important and necessary. Humans lived to work and vice versa. High school and college educations were merely stepping-stones not only for psychological fulfillment, but to make a buck in order to eat, live long,

and prosper. Working and contributing to
society was damn important back in the day!
However, many older people got so defined-by
and entangled in their professions/careers that
when retirement came over them, they were
ill-prepared to handle it. There is no choice
about getting old, yet some forget how to live
with themselves now that there is more time
to worry. Enter hobbies and distractions. "All
work and no play makes Jack a dull boy" was a
sardonic but wise axiom that my young
friends and I embodied to cultivate "lives"
outside of teenaged education. Sports were the
main outlets for doing something exciting and
different. Other pals chose art, woodworking,
hunting and fishing as constructive outlets
that hopefully would last a lifetime. After the
exhaustive, middle-age, money-hungry,
parenting, tuition-paying, marital-squabbling
years were blissfully over, I slowly but surely
returned to my former "fun" endeavors and
rekindled my love of entomology, writing,

athletics, etc. I now have more time to embrace my former hobbies and pastimes. However, sometimes I have to habitually remind myself to get off my dusty ass and actually engage in them! Anyway, and unfortunately, many of my close buddies, due to boredom or depressing health issues, began to indulge in distracting vices such as gambling and alcohol/drug abuse. Why not, right? The retired lot earned their earthly rewards, dammit; leave them alone for Christ's sake. Now, I'm no judge or jury as to the lifestyles of the geriatric set but going nuts in old age may indeed be appropriate. Fuck being more productive! You can't take it with you, remember? Senior senility and senescence are real and maybe trying to keep working is facetious foolishness. There might be nothing wrong by regularly boarding a huge bus with other cannabis consuming, cane-wielding, gun-toting, retirees and getting bussed to glitzy casinos to unload loot in exchange for a few expensive thrills. Previously addictive behaviors, good or bad, can often become magnified in retirement and might be the logical conclusion to a life well-lived or one that was not lived at all. I'd like to end this story with a cautionary tale for my fellow old-timers but cannot. Who am I to extoll a certain lifestyle? All I can say is, "Moderation, if possible. Or not."

18

Pills are Us

How ironic that Hottie Blondie and I, both retired pharmacists, now consume the same life-giving drugs that we once doled out in spades? I recall my days of diligently dispensing medicines and intelligently counseling patients on over-the-counter and prescription pharmaceuticals. Some people say that I was a decent druggie, I mean druggist, back in the day, but I only stuck it out for a very short term. Then I moved on to dental school and dentistry. However, my wife kept counting capsules and compounding confections on the "bench" for a long time before abdicating from the profession because of ongoing chain-store bullshit. Anyway, those halcyon days are over. Today my wife dutifully arranges her personal, daily tablets in a special, plastic, pill organizer box and I get mine ready as well, to be swallowed whole as if part of a ritualistic nightly dessert. But pills keep seniors going dammit; they even keep some retirees alive! Many retired folks would be a passing obituary if not for modern medicine and all the multi-colored medicaments that are part of it. The song *White Rabbit*, by Jefferson Airplane, with the first two lines mentioning pills that make you large and small, is a veiled reference to the original hipsters of the sixties and their psychedelic drug experimentations. Too bad that most of the medicines that seniors take are not for LSD-inspired, mind-bending purposes. Oh well. Of course, with the advent and legalization of pot in all its forms, if old hearts can handle the racing, and feeble minds the paranoia, then have at it. However, I can't take it anymore, literally. Today's weed is way too much for me. The percentage of THC per bone is much too HIGH. What happened to the 3% max per doob? Back in the late seventies, you could party all night, pass around tons of joints, not pass out, not get reefer madness, and still make the college Inorganic Chemistry lecture the next morning. I was formerly an avowed aficionado and a petty, part-time dealer of the *herb* in my *cool*, college *daze*. Seed-removed Columbian Gold and Hawaiian rolled blunts wrapped in Bambú paper (not E-Z Wider, Zig-Zag, or Joker) were sold and blazed up regularly. And nightly bong hits also kept me relatively sane during an insanely difficult undergraduate college tenure. And let's not forget about the cubes of hashish wrapped in aluminum foil that were peddled for six dollars a gram. And, yes, in case you were wondering, my brilliant senior-year pharmacy college roommate and I possessed a stolen, college-issued, pharmaceutical-grade scale that made our paltry and amateurish "drug trade" legit. Nevertheless, my "illicit" notoriety went a long way and gained me many friends in

HIGH places, and I reveled in it. My toking did not affect my grades and my *hot* girlfriend (whom I married) thought HIGHLY of me, too. Score! Now she and I gaze at one another through our coke bottle-thick reading glasses as we sorrowfully reminisce while separately doling out our medications. But they are prescription tablets or capsules and not marijuana-infused gummies. How poignantly funny, but sad. Anyhow, staying metabolically healthy, even if slightly overweight, is the new focus of our fitness and diet-obsessed culture. It's not good enough to weeble-wobble around with a walker or crutch anymore. No, today's retirees are shamelessly being goaded to ask their doctors about drug ads as seen on TV and to participate in societal "wellness rituals," like having a YMCA life membership. Why can't oldsters pop a longevity pill to avoid the treadmill of physical fitness? Most retirees already successfully got off the forty-hour-per-week hamster wheel called WORK, exhaled deeply, and looked forward to a nice long rest. They weren't especially looking forward to a new chapter filled with kip-ups and dumbbells just to keep going! I also read somewhere that a good judge of spryness and a subsequent long lifespan is the ability to quickly get up off the ground without using your hands. I guess I should have died twenty years ago. Anyway, I feel let down by all the former and continuing hype of simple solutions to life's extension that's just around the corner. Like the side-effect-free anti-fat pills and jetpacks that were promised and never materialized, I sincerely sympathize with seniors who are somewhat dubious at embarking on an overly strenuous and ludicrous program of exercise if the expiration date has already been pre-stamped on their worn-out bodies. But what about cutting-edge cancer and cardiac treatments, new-fangled vaccines, the burgeoning field of gerontology, gene therapies, stem cell infusions, Crispr gene editing, etc.? Surely they are life-saving modern medical miracles, however, none seem to reliably extend human lives past one hundred years. Betty White and my own, mean-spirited, stubborn, maternal Grandma Olena tried and failed to become centenarians. When your time is up, it's up, although medical issues often hasten the departure. The 36 billion-dollar-gym, health, and fitness industry is raking in big bucks and is ubiquitous while old and gullible buffoons are painstakingly partaking in it as if part of a religious rite. But maybe that's good in a way. What else have the old and weak got to do besides eat too much, sleep too little, drink Wild Turkey, worry incessantly about kids and finances, and then kick off? My wife and I TRY to eat right, do Reiki on each other, work-out moderately, play some sports, and TRY not to become too anxious or overwhelmed by our deteriorating physical and psychological states. So my body is banged up and refuses to listen to me on most days and my mental acuity and acumen are not what they once were. So what. And I take some pills for my ills. So what. I can still piss in a pot without missing the bowl and read the funnies in the morning paper, even when upside down; the paper that is, not me. I'm good, I think.

19

Out of Kilter

I tend to laugh whenever I pass by my unevenly balanced clothes dryer that has somehow managed to shift its load and starts to noisily clunk away while valiantly attempting to dry my soggy sneakers. However, when I think of my upcoming and typical days ahead, I stop chuckling. As already mentioned here and there, merely waking up in the morn and staying upright may be a victory for some retirees, but not necessarily for all. What happened to all the fun we used to have, to compensate for the nonstop stressors of life? And the mindful calmness and confidence that was previously and effortlessly exuded, not brought on by popping Zoloft or Prozac medicaments? What happened? Ha, those bygone days are gone with the wind! As youngsters we played a lot and worked very little. In middle age, those two opposing lifestyles became somewhat equal. In old age, the balance has seemingly swung to the "old grind" again, yet retired seniors are working less or not working at all. So, what gives? Well, this has been a tough one for me to handle and write about. Why do some senior citizens have such a hard time dealing with the rigors of old age? I should know, but I have no easy answers. Is it just aging in general? Unlike flippantly telling someone who is down in the dumps to take a vacation or to sign up at a health club, how do you tell the elderly to stop getting old? And is that all it is? The logical traumatic and dramatic ending to a good beginning? Man, like Captain Kirk cleverly used to do, I've willfully evaded and ducked death as much as humanly possible. However, that has not prevented my body and mind from slowly withering away. And all the mental positivity, wellness check-ups and self-help books are not really helping to reverse my constantly assaulted finances or the descent into irreversible somnolence, senescence, and obsolescence. And then my *hot* and usually cheerful wife removes the overheated track shoes from the stopped dryer, smirks in my general direction, and reminds me that my foul moods are catching and to stop being such a ding-dong. What a gal, what a gal! Is that one of the reasons why I married her, for her to gently but firmly call out my many flaws and to have me stop endlessly obsessing about my diet and so-called life? Nearly forty-plus married years later and I guess her advice is still working. But, regardless, I continually feel the need to regain that balance of work/play I used to have. Perhaps I should embody that famous demotivational saying from the 1979 movie *Meatballs* - "It Just Doesn't Matter"- and use it as my New Age mantra. Or maybe I should get over myself, accept my many fallibilities, and become more consumed with getting laid rather than getting the never-ending bills paid. There will ALWAYS be "debts" to pay, monetary and otherwise. It's time to start living, dammit! Perhaps my wife has a good point and hopefully will keep me pointing in the right erection, I mean direction.

20

Use it or Lose it

I'm not talking about private parts that may have retired somewhat in retirement. No, I'm speaking of something even more deleterious. Yes, it's damn hard to keep up with the horde of passwords, sign-in phrases and credit card fiascos that today's frenetic and fucked-up world demands. You dutifully punch in a well-thought-out thirteen-letter/symbol password followed by carefully created security questions that only you can answer. You are all set forever and come hell or high water, can instantly access the website easily and without much ado. Ha, ha. Not so fast, not so fast, Karen! When was the last time you signed into it? Oh, last month, or last year? Good luck, then! You know the rest of the story – you try in vain to sign-in but have to reset the password first because of inactivity. And when

that fails, you need to answer the three
security questions that you had previously set
up as a failsafe. But wait, your high school
best friend's name was not Steve, you never
lived on Edgerton Street and your first car was
definitely not a 1970, used, olive-green,
Plymouth Valiant. Damn, how stupid of you!
Really? And this has happened numerous
times, to the point where I chuckle warmly
every time "security" questions are involved.
What's the purpose of them if they are useless
in your time of need? Of course, simple emails
or texts cannot be easily sent to knowledgeable
company associates to correct the debacle.
And toll-free phone calls keep you on hold
and assume you have unlimited free time. But
you try and call anyway. Finally, the banal
background music stops and a peevish-
sounding representative answers the
telephone, after you have done more pacing
around the house than your dog does in an
entire day. The rep matter-of-factly instructs

you to go back online and reset your password.... When you sarcastically reply that you cannot because of the bogus security questions that you can no longer answer, there is usually silence at the other end of the blower. The manager then gets involved and "magically" overrides the system, gives you a temporary password, and thanks you for your patronage. Only two hours later you are successfully watching pay-per-view, WWE wrestling again, but anxiously wonder if you answered your own security questions correctly this time around! Oh goody, now it was time to physically assault my bank's ATM and withdraw some cash. Now THAT should be a fairly straightforward transaction, correct? What a joke! When was the last time I used my bank/debit card, I wondered? Three months ago? Of course the glossy card got spit out as the people in line behind me glared and growled at my incompetence and seemingly senior moment. Never mind, a smart-aleck bank associate inside will be able to rectify this "minor" problem in a Jiff. But in lieu of a smooth encounter, the experience turns out to be crunchy peanut butter instead. A good hour into the session, inside a tight and claustrophobic cubicle, the passive-aggressive "interrogation" by the bored bank representative continues: "We have to reset everything. Please retype a new pin number and not the one you previously used. And the user code is not your name anymore. And you cannot reuse that same fifteen-letter-long password either. Oh, and what is your Social Security number?" You know, the one that has been given out so much that even the bank's custodian can repeat it verbatim? I am sweating at this point, frantically cribbing notes, and trying hard to remember all the fresh numerical codes that have been newly assigned. But I grin and bear it although the patronizing and scolding palaver of the young, bank ASSociate makes me feel awful and old.

I'm a dentist, dammit! I have been through much worse in my life, yet this ordeal psychologically hurts me and exposes the underbelly of my overall computer illiteracy. And it was all due to ATM inactivity, and because I wanted a few measly bucks to pay for some measly fowl parts at the fast-food joint across the street from the bank. Well, I missed the ground-up beaks and feet called chicken nuggets and hungrily returned home to lie down after that tiring outing. Credit card fraud and miscommunications are yet another set of stressors that retirees have to deal with, regardless of their seniority status. Scrupulously checking monthly statements, either online or on paper statements, is the surest way to detect spending irregularities. I never bought gasoline at a Stuckey's in Eastaboga, Alabama. What the hell? I had been dutifully "hidin' like Biden" and not motored south from 2020 to 2022. Those were not legitimate charges! Fortunately, VISA quickly straightened out the mess and congratulated me on being so vigilant about the incurred but fraudulent expenses. However, what if I had never bothered to scrutinize my monthly VISA bills? And what if I did not use my credit cards regularly? You have to watch anything and everything, yet as senior citizens, our diminished pea brains and vision have already taken a life-long pounding. Our gooey gray matters have also hitherto been taxed to the max! And now we are asked and tasked to keep up, or else? It is downright impossible I tell you, yet somehow most retirees continue to sally forth. "It's so unfair," as a previous, pompous president often stated. But, so what. Today's retirees are forced to remain sharp and astute and to remember all the things that have to be used in order to keep using them. God help me, if there is one!

21

The Unexpected Avalanche

Seeing and sensing my upcoming retirement was similar to my former competitions in the 100-and 200-meter dashes on the outdoor track and snowshoe sprints on packed snow. All I had to do was maintain proper form and function, keep up my top-end speed and finish strong, running hard through the tape. And I did it, time and again, oftentimes winning the age-group-sanctioned races. And becoming an "official" senior citizen was going to be no different. Well, not exactly. I thought I had all my fuckin' ducks in a realistic row and then suddenly realized that "life" didn't get the memo and really doesn't care. I stupidly assumed that the surrounding hectic world would slow down at the same rate as me. It was arrogant and faulty thinking at its worst. For example, because my income would be less, I falsely assumed the commensurate bills would be smaller too. Also, since my internal energy levels were lower, the grass outside that needed regular mowing would grow less. You get it. However, none of that transpired. Nothing and nobody cooperated with me. The weeds kept right on sprouting and mock me to this day. What the eff? My money and wellness are both decreased yet diligent downsizing has NOT brought the desired outcome I had hoped for. It's hard to live below your means if constant fiscal drainage keeps lowering your monetary mean. Life and its associated expenses keep bum-rushing at me causing undue consternation and worry. I was prepared to take a hit in the wallet, but not to have my appliances, cars, health, home, lawn mowers, etc. continually cry for upgrades and repairs at every turn. It's as if nothing has changed, darn it. And thanks to raging, government-caused inflation, now I have to pay a lot more at the pump, and more

for the same stuff that I just bought yesterday!
Perhaps I should start wearing my orange and
white Whip Inflation Now (WIN) button
which I had received in 1974 from President
Gerald Ford to help fight inflation. However,
it was a cruel political joke perpetrated on
Americans; it didn't work for Ford, and I
doubt it will currently work either! Not to
continue griping, but the unexpected
avalanche of increased payments for goods
that HAVE to be periodically purchased
because of planned obsolescence is
breathtaking. You gotta buy a brand new,
foreign-made, and more expensive washer if
your "new" one just conked out. What are you
going to do, make the old lady wash your
holey tighty-whities down by the local creek
in subzero temperatures? Sorry, I can't believe
I said that! Anyway, I wasn't prepared to "fix"
so many expensive items on a fixed income!
The upside is I now have more time to swear,
fart, burp, and complain out loud, although in

the confines of my house and yard. So, what are the solutions? Retiring with a bigger nest egg, but only if the stock market cooperates? Raising more greenbacks by becoming a slum landlord and unscrupulously gouging hapless tenants? Re-entering the workforce as a gig-worker, Uber driver, or toothless Kmart greeter (ten stores are left)? All of the above? Anyhow, it seems as though the technological gadgets and gizmos we live with have to be "watered and fed" on a daily basis. My hard-earned money appears to flow out unimpeded just so I can barely stay alive in the so-called modern world. And yet, my finances are finite as a senior citizen. As a frustrated knee-jerk reaction, perhaps I should sell it all and move to cheaper and greener pastures like many retired folks and smart Delaware County cows have done? Or maybe I should just pull up my socks, take a hard swipe at that honey-do list, and recalculate my dubious spending habits? Now I do all three no matter how tiring it is.

And hopefully I will not fall off the ladder while fixing my leaking rain gutters for the umpteenth time. In addition, I'll try hard to silence my anxious inner critic while ruefully ruminating over the elevated eaves on my house and the elevated consumer price index. Nice thoughts!

22

Outliers

Not to be confused with outright liars, although there may be some similarity between the two groups, elderly outliers are a confounding lot. Let me explain. Granted, there are, and always have been, media advertisements showcasing phony, fit, trim, older actors/actresses trying to get stupid dupes to buy something or other. However, while most commercial images are indeed fake in order to give seniors false hope while absconding with their money, there is some truth to "youthful aging." While I was laid up after my second arthroscopic right knee surgery during my very late '50s, I chanced upon a local newspaper article that piqued my interest and revolted me at the same time. There I was moaning, groaning and feeling sorry for myself while an eighty-eight-year-old man had recently picked up road racing and was suddenly winning all the local events in his Jurassic age group. His knees were fresh and not worn out like mine after a 50-plus-year competitive amateur career of punishing singles tennis. No, his bony joints were finally ready to do some running, all happy and lubricated with gobs of pumping synovial fluid, unlike mine which were seizing up due to arthritis and wear and tear. Was that the secret? Don't needlessly wear yourself out too early in life? And does that sentiment include my deceased PATERNAL Grandpa Petro and MATERNAL Grandma Olena? I never thought my live-in Estonian grandparents were that special, but they each managed to spitefully keep on living to a very old age. Both were unfortunate Displaced Persons (WWII war refugees) yet enjoyed long American lives in healthy and youthful states. They had similar old-world upbringings and vile and nasty dispositions, which may have contributed to their defiance of death. They aggravated the shit out of each other, my parents, my sister, and me, yet continually lived to talk about it. But besides good fortune, like never getting life-threatening illnesses or being run over by a quiet EV, what was the real lowest common denominator that influenced their long lives besides their respective, acidic personalities? Or are there any? Maybe not. And can retirees glean something from those "forever young" babes such as Christie Brinkley, Elizabeth Hurley, and Bo Derek, or are their unique chromosomal telomeres just more firmly attached than ours? I don't know and science does not have ready answers, at least not yet. Unfortunately, most seniors cannot do anything about their genetic make-ups, regardless of all the Reiki, Pilates, and mindful breathing exercises that are willfully and purposely executed. Perhaps we can't do anything about our bodies at all? Perhaps all that mind over matter chatter is hogwash and a big hunk of hooey? I was woefully cogitating as I laid down the newspaper and then reflected some more. I thought about the ironic answers given by TV-interviewed oldsters regarding their supposed secrets to a lengthy lifespan. Each one had daily "rituals" that she/he swore by. Some still drank whisky and rye, some continued to smoke dope, and others ate candy corn nightly. Come on! The takeaway was puzzling, stultifying, and humorously taxing. It was obvious that there were no obvious answers. And no confidences were revealed, just facetiously joking replies and amazing survival stories. Some of the questioned had endured extremely stressful war experiences while others had faced starvation and deprivation - all events that were unwittingly forced upon them. Yet all were still alive and kicking. Of course, one can chalk up all of life as something we truly don't understand and part of a grand design by a higher power. It's possible and I don't completely discount that kind of assumptive reasoning, but it may be a false assumption, nevertheless. Anyway, I say bravo to all those super seniors who continually lace up their running flats to go jogging instead of making recurrent trips to doctors' offices and drug stores to procure life-extending procedures and prescriptions, respectively. Or can those modalities be mutually congruent? Could be. Maybe that's why some people CAN run around as they age. They relentlessly and dutifully visit physicians and take pills to enable them to get their thrills! Anyhow, I convalesced and regained most of my knee power again, however, I sadly had to discontinue playing my beloved tennis. Oh well, I'm still hitting pickleballs and ping pong balls and am grateful to be moving when "racing" about on a much smaller court and around an even smaller table tennis table. And I try not to think too much about all those obnoxious and spunky retirees that make me look and feel badly. Perhaps I am one of them at this point? I try to stay physically active and young at heart even though long in the tooth. Yet oftentimes the thought of being a healthy geriatric outlier can best be summed up by that familiar phrase: better lucky than good!

23

Stress

Everyone gets it and everyone feels it. Some scientists say that it is actually good for humans, in small doses that is. Unfortunately, I cannot readily pontificate about the various stresses or "get after it," like unblinking liberal blowhard Chris Cuomo used to say while still employed by CNN, because I am eminently not qualified to do so! However, I can at least offer up my two or three cents. Mental stress and inherent anxieties have already been touched upon in this volume. While many retirees seem to showcase an abatement and mellowing of inborn neuroses, in others, the opposite occurs. And while most seniors handle unexpected external stressors rather routinely, some continually suffer from and despise them. Different strokes for different folks, I guess, and different coping strategies as well. It all depends on each person's mental machinations and aggrievement tolerances. Notwithstanding, I will end this ditty not by arrogantly claiming to have overcome my own insecurities and nerves or by offering ludicrous tone-deaf tonics, but by lightly mentioning some observations. Is stress and the reactions to it caused by nature or nurture? Is a person born hard-wired anxious or was the resultant nervousness caused by parents, upbringing, and environment? Who knows? But does it really matter? I don't think so. However, if you bit your fingernails as a kid, you most likely will continue to do so as a senior citizen, or at least sublimate that nervy habit into drinking, smoking, or worse. Well, whoop-dee-doo, as Archie Bunker often said. In other words, stress can be acknowledged, but rarely successfully conquered, no matter from whence it came or how bodily toxic it can become. So, should retirees take a hint out of Aldous Huxley's dystopian book *Brave New*

World and self-medicate themselves with booze, pot, and pills to soothe and assuage the onslaught of magnified bodily and mental ills? Maybe, but perhaps there are other ways of managing the ravages of anxious aging without extended suicide. I have touched upon and preached about the value of having satisfying hobbies, productive habits and other such snively drivel from atop my soapbox and supposed high horse, but I have no real answers. I have also been a captive slave to low-level general anxiety my entire life. Sports, spouses, supplements, drugs, and death are sometimes called "cures" for unrelenting nervousness, even in old age. Ha! Is there hope AND humor in that last statement? I sincerely hope so.

24

Pros and Cons

The day finally arrived as you packed up your papers, pictures, and plants, and happily exited the office for the last time. Fanciful thoughts of increased travel and sexual trysts danced in your head as you looked forward to retirement. What a joke! Being retired is a lot like that seminal scene from the 1989 flick *When Harry Met Sally*, as Sally tearfully laments that a previous boyfriend had promised her spontaneous trips to Rome and sex on the kitchen floor – neither of which materialized. Many senior citizens greatly look forward to frisky frivolity, money flowing in regularly without being worked for, and upcoming adventures. Alas, many of those farcical daydreams do not come to fruition, at least not in the way that was painstakingly planned for in a youthful mind's eye.

Oftentimes hash pipe dreams go up in vapid smoke and never fully materialize when the stark realities of growing old kick in. But, certainly the pros of retirement outweigh the cons. Or do they? Grandiose expectations and failing mental and physical health can ruin a perfectly good retirement, regardless of more time availability! "Wherever you go, there you are," is a well-worn axiom attributed to various past sages and two-bit, armchair philosophers. To most people it means that you can't get away from who you really are, whether in Belize, Bimini, in your own big backyard, or anywhere else for that matter. Your past and present pains and peccadillos follow you around like damn armadillos. What makes anyone think that retirement will be any different? If you were a nervous Norton before, you will continue to be so. But wait a second. What about the increased time available for rest, recreation, and carnal coitus on the kitchen counter? Well, perhaps, but life

and entropy keep on happening with disorder
rather than order being the norm. The most
recent, pollyannish, feeble and feckless U.S.
presidency comes to mind, one that appeared
to be overwhelmed with realistic problems
that could not be solved with idealistic
solutions. It was one unmanageable crisis after
another. However, most of the resultant
failures were self-inflicted wounds. But unlike
dysfunctional government flunkies, most
savvy seniors can distinguish between idealism
and realism, and act accordingly. But it can
become difficult to change one's stripes. Sure,
there seem to be more hours to finally get
things done around the house or to go on that
coveted road-trip, but can you and will you
enjoy those things as pre-planned? Unexpected
crapola keeps hitting retirees with the same
frequency as when they were youngsters. The
difference is that most young people can
handle the downturns better. I recall having
had just as much angst, anger and downright

bad juju happen to me in my twenties as I do now. However, either I resolved the issues or shrugged them off, and I still had enough mental compartmentalization skills and energy available to live the best life I could. Pharmacy college, dental school, paying taxes, making car and mortgage payments, marriage, children, etc. were seemingly juggled effortlessly. Of course, my brain was relatively new back then and free of clutter and cognitive cobwebs. Unfortunately, old galoots are called that for a reason! Seniors tend to be a bit slower, and the honey-do list becomes a bit longer. And the constant circuitous maintenance of "time-saving appliances" becomes a labor of unrequited hate. Additionally, what about the obligations and responsibilities that never went away? I have the time to do nothing now, so why am I wasting it mowing my three acres twice weekly, and then repeatedly having the blasted mowers fixed? I find myself as stupidly busy as before, darn it. Surely, I could hire someone for the "odd" jobs that keep rearing their ugly heads but old quirks, such as my perfectionist tendencies and saving money, die hard. And I'm sure archaic, elderly cavemen had it just as bad, if they even lived to a ripe old age. I'm sure there was something for even a toothless and useless Neanderthal to do such as starting or putting out a fire, skinning an elk carcass or clubbing a nosy neighbor. Did a stooped and decrepit Homo Erectus watch the deer and the antelope play while sitting in a rocking-stone chair on a stone stoop? Did he ever kick back and mindfully meditate while thinking about the good old days? Ha, ha, I think not; I'm not talking about the Flintstones. There are always planned and unplanned deeds that need to be reckoned with, age notwithstanding. There is no time for goldbricking or for rhetorical reflections to bubble up to the surface. But if there finally is more time to take stock of life and to forcefully ruminate on the resultant regrets, so what? The past has passed; it's time to put that black and white photo album away and tell Alexa to turn on the coffee pot and brew some Death Wish Coffee. My father's retirement fantasy was to buy "something small" in Juno Beach, Florida, go surf fishing, and play tennis daily. In that hallucinatory vision, he would be all set. Newly retired, relatively healthy and athletic, he was ready and able to make the move to the sunny "promised land" and live out his version of the American dream. It never happened. Pop, although brilliant, had not thought through a few IMPORTANT things such as my mother's recalcitrance to moving and about the pitfalls of possessing out-of-state real estate. His lofty illusions were effectively squelched, dag nab it! "You are not going to go fishing every day and leave me alone in some tiny, cramped apartment," I heard Mom whisper on more than one occasion whenever I visited them. "You could

come along and fish all day with me," he
would counter as she rolled her eyes. Yeah,
right! So, they stayed securely anchored in
their dink-hole, rural village in Upstate New
York. But Pop did end up playing doubles
tennis with his local cronies whenever he
could, right up until he passed. But even
before he died, he would occasionally bring up
the subject of having missed the Florida-boat,
and about how happy he would have been
whiling away his time casually catching
Whiting, Bluefish, and Pompano while
standing barefoot on the sun-kissed beach.
Mom wasn't a Debbie Downer, but wanted to
remain relatively close to my sister and me and
had no delusions about living a "different,"
air-conditioned kind of life in the South now
that she was also retired. Plus, she really knew
him after sixty-plus years of matrimony. She
knew that it was escapist thinking on his part
and would never come to fruition. However,
many of their brave retired professor friends

did take the plunge and drove off to a warmer, southern climate. Some loved it, and some eventually returned home. I guess my conservative parents could have at least become *snowbirds* and dipped their beaks into the warm Atlantic. But who would have watched their home for three or four months while they were gone? What was the point of getting away if they would be worried sick about their precious domicile the whole time? And since Mom and Dad could not reconcile those questions, they never left their secure and dusty settlement. C'est la vie. They had sampled Florida on many vacation trips, but ultimately stayed firmly planted in Bumfuck, N.Y. However, I think the biggest con job of a "happy" retirement is declining physical and mental health. Toward the end, my dad would incessantly stew about politics, which he took personally, as well as all the things he could have said or done differently. And now he was going downhill physically too. However, I lovingly applaud him for sticking it out for ninety-plus years, always chronically cynical and on the lookout for "bad things" that were bound to happen. And they did. Sometimes, you get what you ask for. His kind of misplaced and worrisome paranoia reminds me of that 1976 horror classic *The Sentinel,* where the female lead is ultimately tasked with protecting the world from evil. It was her "preordained job" to wait and watch as a sentinel, to make sure that devilish minions did not escape from Hell and wreak havoc on the world. However, no one forced my dad to worry so much or so profoundly. Many of the supposed happy perks of retirement escaped him. Well, he did have some fun occasionally fishing for sunfish and pickerel in a local lake and habitually chasing tennis balls around on the cracked high school and college courts. But as he unhealthily aged, he was fond of exclaiming, "Now, what?" every time there was an unpleasant upheaval in his life or an unexpected expense to reckon with. As he grew sicker in retirement, he wanted his life to be copacetic and not as acerbic as it often turned out to be. But he had one secret weapon that prevented him from descending into despondency and that was: hope. And that one word may have been the most important driver of his life and ensuing longevity. Eternally optimistic, although you would never know it, Dad could rant and rave about the unfairness of life and then in the same troubled breath look forward to the next day. All in all, his thought-processes were part of a dichotomous existence that my mom, sister, and I accepted. And, similar to his elderly devolution, I often find myself resembling a primitive paramecium or amoeba. I instinctively recoil from noxious stimuli and move away from many physical projects and perceived-as-fun activities, even though there are now seemingly more hours on the ever-ticking clock for "enjoyment." I still participate in long-term hobbies, competitive sports, and consensual, non #MeToo, heterosexual sex with the same old lady, but continually fret about life's bullshit as per usual. And insidious memory slippage is a real thing! Where the fuck are those twenty pairs of reading glasses that I squirreled away around the house just in case of trouble? You know what I mean? Now don't get me wrong, it's great being retired, but facetious gratefulness and appreciation only go so far. Insincerely spouting off gratuitous gratitude while faking it may not work out in the long term. Because even in retirement there is always something that irks me, something that needs to be fed, attended to, repaired, replaced, and worried about. You know, *tings dat mek yuh tire*, as one would say in the Caribbean Patois tongue. But that's just me. In conclusion, do the pros outweigh the cons as aging occurs or is it the other way around? I don't know. All I know is that crotchety,

LGBTQXYZ-challenged, old dogs like me still have to get up out of the patio lounge chair, stand up, put down that frosty pint of Natty Daddy, and clean the grill every time it is used. You know, the cons never truly go away. My wife wonders if I will continue to get wound up at every tired turn and keep on whining forever; or will I get better with age like fine wine? As if.... Can't even....

25

Last Words

Hopefully this book was not an overly depressive diatribe. Conceivably it was a comedic, though unvarnished, look at aging and all its triumphs and tribulations. Everyone has mental and physical battles going on, even the elderly. Living in general is often compounded by uninvited and disturbing experiences that often continue or become magnified upon retirement. And forget about having more time for anything. It seems to speed up just when retirees wish it to slow down! Consequently, I tried to humorously highlight some age-old absurdities, but without delving too deeply into the suffering and anguish associated with losing loved ones, funds, food, shelter and lastly, one's sense of self. As a youngster, I was fearlessly chomping at the proverbial bit to get older, to get on with life, and achieve the "pledged" payoff. Now I want to decelerate time in order to savor the past and present. However, I only tepidly look forward to the future because I have already witnessed and personally experienced more failures than successes. In addition, a lifetime of threats, existential and otherwise, have contributed to my often bleak and oblique observations. Examples include the deadly Chinese pestilence, domestic "transitory" hyperinflation (yeah, right!), and the unprovoked Russian attack on Ukraine - all unwanted and unwarranted events that were recently foisted upon us. The hits keep right on coming, n'est-ce pas? I reached the point of "Aggravation Saturation" years ago, yet that two-word phrase continually haunts and taunts me. Thusly, and rightly or wrongly, I've started to treat people the same way they treat me. Just sayin'. Some people say that I have become a bitter old prick and am no longer the same bon vivant and *dirty white boy* of yesteryear. Tru dat! Furthermore, no one told me that getting old meant less and not more of everything, except for bills, ills, and spills – those seem to have multiplied! To wit, my high expectations and the supposed freedom from work and worry that retiring promised were woefully misguided ideals and to date have not fully materialized. Lastly, and I am unanimous in this, hopefully retirement is more than dreaming of Florida and facetiously trumpeting phony gratitude while barely breathing. Should I optimistically exalt when nothing "bad" happens? Should I indeed celebrate each day as if it's my last? Perhaps, but there must be more to retired senior-living, although....

Anyway, were my humorous sentiments and colorful verbiage mostly a self-deprecating case of unanticipated sour grapes? Probably. But were they also a realistic accounting of life in general? "Why soitenly!" as Curly would say.

Hopefully, the cynical and twisted reflections of a jaded, dental dotard touched a nerve, but also brought out some heartfelt guffaws in the process. Nevertheless, as all good things that must come to an end, it may be time to fold up my old and tattered, "comical" circus tent and do the reading world a big favor by fading away into retired obscurity. Or not!

Thanks for the read.

About the Author

Dr. I Mayputz (not his real name) graduated with highest honors from high school, pharmacy college and summa cum laude from dental school. After completing a master's degree in prosthodontics at a then prestigious institution, he embarked on his dental career in private practice. He once briefly toyed with the idea of earning a Ph.D. to become an actual entomologist, but ultimately decided on a dreadfully stressful, albeit lucrative, livelihood instead. In addition to being an elite master's athlete, published verbal artist, naturalist, and part-time naturist, he is also known as a caustic wit and provocateur. Dr. I. Mayputz has released many nature articles in regional journals under his real name. Additionally, he has authored multiple pharmaceutical and dental abstracts as well as written numerous salty children's books, also under his given name. Lastly, he wrote this book to entertain family, old friends, and any curious sod willing to *see* the writing on the wall.

For more alleged levity by Dr. I. Mayputz, please read:

Dental School: A Bizarre Comedy
Pharmacy College: Crazy Daze and Hazy Nites
Elementary School: Wits and Twits
Junior High: The Muddle Years
High School: Buffoonery Central
Dental Delirium: A Humorous Look at Dentistry

WHO
DAT?